AN AMISH ROMANCE

JAMES ROBERTS

Edited by
JAMES ROBERTS
Illustrated by
JAMES ROBERTS

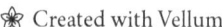

"I dedicate this book to the world in hopes that their relationships are loving and without prejudice"

CONTENTS

INTRODUCTION

This book is a short story of undying love between a man and a woman from entirely different walks of life and how it doesn't affect, but rather strengthens the romance they share.

PREFACE

"Come here. May I put my arm around your waist?"

"Well, I, I,.."

"Look at me Delilah."

"Paul, I don't...Paul I am not...Paul...," says Delilah as Paul places his lips on hers and gently parts his lips in a kiss.

'Delilah?"

"Paul, what? Paul, what just happened?"

"I kissed you Delilah. I am falling in love with you."

"Paul, I don't know what to say."

"Say what you feel, Delilah."

THE INVITATION

"*H*ey Delilah, would you like to come over to my home this weekend for my party?" asks Linda.

"Oh I don't know. What is a party? What do you do at a party?"

"I forgot you don't know about some of the things we do."

"So, is this party with your brothers, sisters, and mama and papa?" asks Delilah.

"No, silly! Parents aren't allowed."

"Why not?"

"Because we have boys coming to my party," says Linda.

"What do you mean, Linda? Why can't you have your mama and papa at your party with boys?"

"Oh Delilah, you don't know why? Come to the party and you will find out."

PAUL

"*P*aul, are you able to come to my party this weekend?"

"I don't know Linda. I assume it is one of those parties you typically have. I don't have anyone I would like to bring with me to the party."

"Come on Paul. I am sure you will find someone at the party. Besides, I invited Delilah."

"You invited Delilah? What did she say? Does she know anything about your parties?"

"She thinks it is one of those family things. She is so naive."

"Give her a chance, Linda. It is not her fault she does not know such things. She has been sheltered most of her life growing up to sixteen years of age. Are you sure it is a good idea exposing her to those things? What boy is she bringing with her?"

'I don't know, maybe her brother."

"Come on Linda, she wouldn't bring her brother if she knew about your parties."

"OK, Paul. You make sure you come to my party. It will be your job to show her 'the ropes'."

"I don't know, Linda. I hardly know her."

"Paul, don't you think she is pretty?"

"Well, I wouldn't describe her as pretty. She is cute, but she is only sixteen, you know?"

"Oh, I forgot about her age. Well, come to my party. You can keep her company, at least."

JEDEDIAH

"Delilah, what are you going to be doing this weekend?"

"Linda invited me to a party at her house?"

"A party? What is a party?"

"I am not sure Jedediah. She said boys are invited. Would you like to come with me to the party?"

"I don't know, Delilah. The other boys I met asked me to go bowling with them."

"Bowling? What is that?"

"I guess it is a type of game. They said something about throwing a ball at something they call pins."

"Well, I suppose I can go alone. We have to learn about the things they do in their culture."

PAUL MEETS DELILAH

"*H*ello, Delilah, I am glad you are here. I was afraid you wouldn't take me up on my invitation to the party," says Linda.

"I wanted to bring my brother, but he is going to play a game called bowling."

"That is OK, here are some of my friends I want you to meet. Hey guys, this here is Delilah. She is new to the area. This is Tom and Joan, John and Linda, Tammy and Joe, and Paul."

"Hello, I am pleased to meet you all," says Delilah.

"Linda, come over here. What is with that girl Delilah?" asks Tom.

"What do you mean?"

"Why is she dressed like that? Where did she come from? Her dress is all pale blue and down to her ankles."

"Tom, it is her culture. Maybe Joan can talk with her and get her interested in some more modern clothes."

"Linda, why did you invite Delilah to this party? How old is she?" asks Tammy.

"She is sixteen," says Linda.

"Sixteen? Wouldn't you think she is too young for this? Jailbait?" asks Tom.

"I talked to Paul and he is going to keep her company," says Linda.

"Does Paul know her age?" asks Joan.

"Paul, I want to introduce you to Delilah. She is new in our neighborhood. Why don't you show her around," says Linda.

"Hello, Delilah. It is nice to meet you. Would you like something to drink? Some punch maybe?" asks Paul.

"No thank you. I wouldn't mind some water, though."

"So, Delilah, where do you come from?" asks Paul.

"I live in the small town of Cato."

"Cato? I believe most of those people are Amish. Are you Amish, Delilah? You are dressed like they dress."

"Yes, I am from the Amish Community there."

"You can actually travel out of your Community and come to parties like this?"

"Yes, me and my brother are on *Rumspringa*."

"What is that Delilah?"

"When an Amish child reaches the age of sixteen, he or she is given the chance to leave the Community and experience your culture. In this way, we have the opportunity to leave the Community permanently and live in your community if we like what we experience."

"So, this has been the first few days of your escape; you and your brother?"

"Yes, and I must say you live an entirely different life than us. It is hard for me to get used to your busy lifestyle. How do you ever get anything done; you have so much to do in a day."

"How is your culture different than ours?" asks Paul.

"Other than having horse and buggy for travel, we rise in the morning and help our mama with her chores and then travel out to the barn to tend to the animals. Some days we may go with our mama and papa to market. Usually in the afternoon, the young children play out in the yard, either tossing a ball, or hide and seek; you know, those types of fun."

"Do you go out and work? Do you have a job?" asks Paul.

"No, not a job like you have. We tend to the sale of baked goods and blankets at our roadside stands. The girls in our Community learn to sew at an early age and the boys learn to farm."

DELILAH'S RESCUE

"*H*ey Paul, are you going to talk all night, you cradle robber?" Get to it! There is an empty bedroom up there. Be careful, she's a young one, you know!" exclaims Tom.

"Paul, what is he talking about?" asks Delilah.

"Oh, never mind him. Let us go up to that room. It is too noisy down here and I don't want to hear any more of their taunting," says Paul.

"Paul, really, tell me what is going on here. Where did everyone go? I hear lots of noise coming from those other rooms. I hear girls moaning and whimpering. Are they all right?"

"Delilah, come over here and sit down on the bed next to me and I will explain. Please close the door. You see, Linda has this party lots of times and well, do you know about…well you know."

"No, Paul, I don't know."

"Delilah, what happens in your Community when a girl marries?"

"The woman cleaves to her husband and they begin to make a life together helping each other."

"Is that all, Delilah?"

"Well, in time they have children to raise."

"How do they get their children?"

"I really don't know, Paul. Somehow it just happens."

"Delilah, do you know what happens when a man and woman cleave in bed?"

"I guess so. I think it is when the *bundling board* is removed from the bed."

"What is a *bundling board*, Delilah?"

"It is a board in the bed to separate the boy from the girl before marriage, so they don't touch each other inappropriately."

"Well, the parties Linda has, involves beds with the *bundling board*, as you call it, removed so …"

"Do you mean the boys here at this party, can touch the girls in the beds?"

"Yes, and they do more than that," says Paul.

"Is that why you brought me to this room and asked me to sit next to you on this bed?"

"No, Delilah. Please sit down. I am not going to touch you. I just wanted to get you out of the area where we are being taunted."

"What is a cradle robber, Paul?"

"It is what they call a guy who is with a girl at a young age such as you. In our culture, you are considered underage to be touched by a boy. It is illegal."

"Illegal?"

"Yes, a guy can be punished for touching a girl under the age of eighteen, in our culture."

"You mean touching as if the *bundling board* is removed from the bed?"

"Yes, Delilah."

"Paul, I would like to leave."

"How did you get here? How will you get to your home?"

"I walked here. My brother and I have an apartment down a way from here."

"Would you mind if I accompany you in your walk to your apartment?"

"That will be fine with me Paul."

TAUNTING PAUL

"Hey Paul, what did you discover under that swatch of cloth she has on? Did you find what you were looking for? I bet you needed a flashlight!" the boys taunt as Delilah and Paul walk to the entrance door of Linda's house.

"Guys leave her alone. Keep your remarks to yourself."

"Sure Paul, sure. She is quite cute. Does that cuteness travel down…?"

"Shut up and leave her alone!" exclaims Paul.

PAUL DISCUSSES WITH DELILAH

"*P*aul, what are they talking about?"

"Pay no attention to them, Delilah."

"No, Paul, if I am going to get used to your culture, I need to know what those guys are referring too. I need to understand your way of speaking in your community."

"Delilah, can we talk about it later? I want to learn more about you and your Community and this walk with you is the perfect opportunity."

"OK, Paul."

"At what age do girls in your Community date and marry?" asks Paul.

"Do you mean when a boy courts a girl?"

"Yes. How does it work in your Community?"

"At my age, a girl can marry. In our culture a girl can marry early in age so to bear many children."

"How many children does a girl you talk about have?"

"As long as the *bundling board* is removed, the children keep coming."

"I see. Are you courting a boy at this time, Delilah?"

"No, I want to live in your culture for a while before I think about being courted."

"It doesn't sound like you should wait too long before courting and marrying."

"Here we are Paul, this is my apartment. I thank you for walking with me. Good night."

"Wait a minute, Delilah. Would you mind having breakfast with me tomorrow morning?"

"I don't know Paul. Is it a normal thing to do in your community?"

"Yes, it is. How about I meet you here tomorrow morning at eight and we will have breakfast."

"OK, how do we have breakfast out here?"

"No, no, we will go to a restaurant to have breakfast."

"Restaurant? What is that?"

"Be out here at eight, Delilah. Good night."

"Good night Paul."

LINDA

"Paul how was it with Delilah?" asks Linda.

"It was fine. She is a sweet girl."

"The guys at the party tonight want to know if you made a 'home run' with her. They said you took her to my parents' bedroom."

"Linda, she is underage and no, I didn't touch her. I didn't plan on touching her either."

"Paul, no one would have told if you 'had your way' with her at sixteen years of age."

"Linda, drop it!"

PAUL, DELILAH AND BREAKFAST

"Good morning Delilah. How was your rest last night?"

"Hi, Paul. I rested very well last night. You must tell me what those guys were talking about last night."

"Sure, Delilah, but let us go and talk about it over breakfast. I am hungry."

"What will you have Delilah. Order anything you want."

"In our Community, we have eggs, bacon or sausage with pancakes, so I will have that."

"So, you want to know what those guys were talking about?" asks Paul.

"Yes, I do."

"When the *bundling board* is lifted from the bed, how does the boy touch the girl?" asks Paul.

"I happened to see a magazine in a store and there were pictures of boys hugging girls very closely and they were not wearing clothes. Some of the pictures showed the guy 'connected' with the girl..." says Delilah.

"Yes, and that is what the guys were referring too."

"I don't understand, Paul."

"The guys wanted to know if we 'connected', up in the bedroom, like the pictures you saw in the magazine."

"Oh, my! Never, no we didn't…noooo…"

"Take it easy, Delilah. Slow down and take a breath."

"Is that what they were doing at the party?"

"Yes, that is kind of what they were doing."

"I have a feeling what I saw has something to do with the wife having children. But those guys were not…they weren't the wife, were they?"

"No, Delilah, those guys were not married to those girls. Let us table this conversation and talk about it later sometime."

"Paul, were you going to do that with me?"

"No, Delilah, it was never on my mind."

"What are you doing today, Paul?"

"I have a job I need to get too in about an hour. How about we take a walk in the park later today, say around four?"

"That will be fine. I am going to see what kind of job I can do. Our Community gave my brother and I a certain amount of money, but It won't last forever."

"How would you like to go to a store and look for some clothes which match those of our tradition?"

"OK, but I don't like the idea of those dresses. I can't show myself like that."

"Are you talking about the shortness of the dresses?"

"Yes. In our Community, we are not to show ourselves like that. It would entice the boys to do wrong things."

"How about we look for some pants?"

"You mean like the boys wear?"

"Yes, it is either those or the dress. There is no other option."

"Oh…"

"Look, let us go and get you some girl pants and blouse top. You will fit in with my tradition and it will help in getting a job."

"Maybe we can talk about what other things I have to do to fit in with your community," says Delilah.

"You bet."

DELILAH SEEKS EMPLOYMENT

"*Y*ou say your name is Delilah?" asks Mr. Sanford.

"Yes, that is my name."

"You are here looking for a job in our Call Center Operations?"

Yes, that is what I would like," says Delilah.

"OK, what is your speed in typing?"

"*Typing*? I don't understand what you mean by *typing*."

"What are your skills on a computer?" asks Mr. Sanford.

"I guess I don't have any skills on a computer…what is that?"

"I am sorry, Miss Delilah, I am afraid I can't offer you a job."

"Thank you Mr. Sanford for taking the time to speak with me."

DELILAH IS FRUSTRATED

"*D*elilah, how did the interview go today?"

"Oh, Paul, it was horrible! I have no computer skills and I don't even know what *typing* is," Delilah says as she starts to cry.

"That's OK, you will find something," says Paul.

"All I have is farming skills and sewing skills. Are there any jobs for those?" asks Delilah.

"Tell you what, I will do some research for you and see if I can find some jobs that fits your skills. Meanwhile, why don't you have dinner with me tonight and let us talk about getting you some training in typing? How would that be?"

"Paul, I would like that, but I think I am taking way too much of your time."

"You let me be the judge of that. I will be by to pick you up at six?"

"OK, but can we walk? I am not comfortable in that automobile of yours," says Delilah.

JEDEDIAH DOES NOT TRUST PAUL

"*D*elilah, maybe we should go back to our Community," says Jedediah.

"I don't know, brother. I agree it is hard to live in this community. I feel we have to take a little more time to adjust."

"Yeah, sis, but neither of us are having luck in finding a job. Our money will run out soon."

"Jedediah, Paul is going to teach me some skills so I can get a job."

"This Paul. Do you trust him sis?"

"I think I can."

"Just remember he isn't our kind, and you shouldn't go liking him."

"Who said I was liking Paul?"

"Come on sis, you are pretty and all, and we have seen what they do in their tradition; boy and girl and all."

"Jedediah, Paul seems to be a gentleman and he isn't like the others. I am not afraid of him."

"Sis don't get a liking to him. You know he can't enter into our Community."

"Well, brother, I am going to get dressed. Paul is taking me out to dinner, and he is going to start teaching me some skills to get a job."

NICKNAMES

"Delilah, you look very nice this evening," states Paul.

"Oh, my outfit is not that great. I went and got this skirt. At least you can see my ankles. That is a start isn't it, Paul?"

"Yes, you look charming Delilah. By the way, I do not know your last name, or should I say your Christian name?"

"It is Yoder, Delilah Yoder."

"Just Delilah Yoder?"

"Delilah Ann Yoder."

"OK, I see. I do like the name Delilah. Do you go by a nickname?"

"What is a nickname?" asks Delilah.

"Oh, you don't know. I should have known. You see, around here in my community we have short names what we call nicknames."

"What is your nickname, Paul?"

"I was afraid you would ask me that. I do not have a nickname; it is just Paul. Take a name like Robert, his nickname would be Bob."

"You have some very strange traditions in your community. So, what would my nickname be?"

"Well, I guess it could be Del or maybe even Lila."

"I don't like those."

"OK, Delilah it is."

"So, what are you suggesting I have for dinner tonight?" asks Delilah.

"You make that decision, Delilah."

"In my Community, women-folk don't make many decisions. The man of the house does that."

"Well, seeing you are here in my community and you are with me, you have the freedom to choose what you would like to eat."

"Paul, I can't get used to the abundance of food you have in your community. There is so much to pick from."

"I can make a suggestion if you would like."

"Yes, I would like that."

"This type of pasta and meat is a good choice."

"Pasta? What is pasta?"

"It is made from a type of grain and the meat is from a cow. The sauce is made from tomatoes."

"OK, I will have that, then."

DELILAH HAS BUTTERFLIES IN HER STOMACH

"Delilah, would you like to come over to my home and learn typing?"

"Oh, I think I would like that, but I must not be with you alone."

"I don't have a *bundling board,* if that is what you mean."

"Paul, I shall not go to your house alone!"

"Delilah, I am just kidding," says Paul as he reaches for Delilah's hand and lightly places his hand on hers.

"Oh, well, I don't know what to say…Paul?"

"Take my hand, Delilah."

"Paul, I, I, I don't know what to say or do…."

"Say what you feel, Delilah."

"I, I, I feel kind of strange in my stomach. It is almost like it has turned upside down."

"Delilah, what if I tell you I am quite fond of you?"

"What does fond mean, Paul?"

"What I am trying to say is I am taking a liking to you, Delilah."

"Well, Paul, I don't know. I, I, never have felt this way before."

"Delilah, would you like to finish off your meal with some ice cream?"

"Yes, I know what ice cream is. My papa always makes ice cream on Sunday nights."

∼

"Thank you, Paul, for the wonderful dinner. I liked that spa, spa…"

"Spaghetti," says Paul.

"Yes, it tasted great!"

"Are you sure you don't want to go to my home and start sharpening your skills?" asks Paul.

"I think not tonight, Paul. I am tired."

"Delilah?"

"Yes, Paul."

"Come here. May I put my arm around your waist?"

"Well, I, I,.."

"Look at me Delilah."

"Paul, I don't…Paul I am not…Paul…," says Delilah as Paul places his lips on hers and gently parts his lips in a kiss.

'Delilah?"

"Paul, what? Paul, what just happened?"

"I kissed you Delilah. I am falling in love with you."

"Paul, I don't know what to say."

"Say what you feel, Delilah."

"Paul, I feel, well I feel like a foolish girl right now, but will you kiss me again?"

Paul pulls Delilah close to him once again and places his arms around her waist and raises his hands up on her back as he lowers his face to hers. Delilah reciprocates and places her arms around Paul's neck and allows him to pull her closer until their lips touch and she parts her lips just as he parts his and their tongues meet in a twirling motion; first his on top of hers and then hers on top of his. Delilah moans subtly as Paul presses his lips onto hers.

"Paul, oh, Paul…, I, I, I didn't, I shouldn't, we shouldn't have done that, should have we?"

"Why Delilah. Didn't you want to kiss me?"

"Well, yes, Paul, I mean…oh, my stomach has flipped, and I don't know what I feel."

"Delilah, I love you."

"Paul, I must go in now. I am tired and…"

"Will I see you tomorrow, Delilah?"

"Yes, or maybe…oh, oh. Yes, I think so."

"Good night Delilah."

"Yes, good night Paul…oh, oh…Paul, one more time?"

DELILAH IS IN LOVE?

"Sis, what is the matter with you? The sweat is running down your face and you are showing a silly grin. Oh, and you are shaking a bit," says Jedediah.

"Oh, it is nothing brother. It is a bit hot outside."

"Delilah, are you falling for that guy, Paul?"

"I am tired Jedediah. I am going to bed. I will see you in the morning."

LINDA PRYS

"$\mathcal{H}$ey Paul, I see you walked Delilah to her apartment last night," says Linda.

"Yes, I did."

"So, are you getting up the nerve to make a 'home run' with her?"

"Linda, is that all you think about?"

"What else to think about. You know she is a young virgin being the Community she comes from."

"Linda, it is none of your business."

"Paul, you had better do it before one of those other guys do it to her. They have been talking."

"Linda, you tell those guys to mind their own business and if they bother her, they will have me to answer to."

"Oh, Paul, you do like her, don't you?"

"Linda, our conversation is over."

PAUL'S PROPOSAL TO DELILAH

"*H*ello, you must be Delilah's brother," says Paul.

"Yes, I am, and you must be Paul?"

"Yes. Is Delilah here?"

"She is in her dressing room. You do know we have different beliefs than yours?"

"Yes, Delilah has been telling me about them."

"What is it you want with my sister?"

"I am here to court her."

"I don't think she…."

"Jedediah, who are you talking to?" asks Delilah.

"It is Paul. He says he wants to court you."

"I will be out in a minute."

"Good morning, Delilah. How was your night?"

"Paul, I was so tired, but I couldn't get my stomach to get right side up."

"Are you OK with last night? I mean did I turn you away from me. How about we go to the park?"

"No, Paul, I am OK. I, I, I, just don't know what to say."

"What do you want to say, Delilah?"

"Why do you say you love me, Paul?"

"I love you Delilah because of who you are and how I feel when I am around you."

"Paul, I don't, well, how can you love me when we are from different communities?"

"I don't care if you are from a different community or tradition from mine. You are here, in my community right now, and that is all that matters to me."

"But Paul, I am not sure I want to stay in your community. Everything is so different, and I do not have the skills to get work. I don't seem to able to be like you or anyone else in your community."

"Delilah, dear, I don't want you to be anything but you; the way you are. I am not asking you to change."

"But, if I choose to go back, I can't take you with me. You will lose me. We shouldn't get so attached."

"What would happen if you went back with a husband?"

"Paul, what do you mean? If I go back, I won't have a husband."

"Delilah, I love you."

"I know, Paul and I, I, I,"

"You what, Delilah?"

"I don't know, I just don't think you should love me. We are so different."

"Delilah, I have a feeling you feel the same about me?"

"Oh, Paul, we mustn't. We mustn't...oh, oh..."

"Delilah, I love you! Let us revisit last night!"

"Paul, I can't, I mustn't, we mustn't, oh, Paul, hold me. Hold me tight and kiss me. Kiss me like last night. Paul, I love you!"

"That wasn't so hard was it? I know you feel the same way about me the way I feel about you."

"But Paul, it can't work. I don't want to hurt you and leave."

"Leave with me."

"But how?" asks Delilah.

"As your husband. Delilah, will you marry me?"

"Paul, I, I, can't! They will not allow it."

"Do you have to go back to your Community? Stay here with me. Make a new life with me, Delilah."

"But Paul, you know nothing about me."

"I know enough about you to be so madly in love with you."

"I don't know Paul. I don't even know if I could give you children."

"That doesn't matter. I love you and if children come, I will love them too."

"Well, I, I..."

"Just say it, Delilah, just say it."

"Well, well, well, yes I will marry you."

"We must ready ourselves and travel to your Community."

"Why, Paul, I already said they will not honor you as my husband."

"In my community, I can't marry one as young as you."

"That is interesting, in our Community, they expect a girl of sixteen to marry so she can bear many children."

JUDGE CONLEY

"Judge Conley, what ruling is there regarding the Amish in our community?" asks Paul.

"What do you mean, Paul?"

"I know in their Community, a girl of sixteen is encouraged to marry."

"What are you getting at?"

"Suppose an Amish girl of sixteen were to marry a guy in our community? Can she do that?"

"Paul, do you have an Amish girl you proposed to?"

"Well, sir, yes sir I have fallen in love with her and she feels the same. We don't think I would be able to marry her in her Community and I do not want to wait two more years to marry her."

"Well, let's see, we don't have any jurisdiction on them, and their laws are their laws, and we don't cross them."

"So, what are you telling me, Judge?"

"Did you ask her to marry you?"

"Well, yes I did."

"That won't work."

"What do you mean?"

"Paul, in order for you to marry her at the age she is now, she will have to marry you."

"I don't follow, Judge."

"It is simple, I hope. She will need to ask you to marry her. She will need to take that initiative for your marriage to be lawful. It is because when she asks to marry you, she is initiating in her laws of her Community and I cannot abridge that."

"Very clever, Judge."

"You are lucky Paul as long as she wants to marry you and I would suggest coming to me for the marriage and not a traditional wedding. I am sorry Paul."

WILL YOU MARRY ME, PAUL?

"*D*elilah, dear, please walk with me to the park."

"What is the matter Paul?"

"Nothing, my dear, but we need to talk."

"Here, sit with me on the bench."

"Paul, I am worried. How can you be my husband?"

"Delilah, do you want to become my wife?"

"Yes, Paul I do. I want to be your wife. I want to marry you."

"I talked to the Judge earlier today."

"Judge, what is a Judge in your community?"

"Well, a Judge is in court and a Judge makes many different types of decisions for people."

"Court?"

"Yes, I will explain what court is in time, but I talked to him about marriage, specifically how I can marry you in my community."

"Oh, and what did he say?"

"He said for us to be husband and wife in my community is for you to ask me to marry you. By doing that you are acting by the laws in your Community which allows you to be married to me at sixteen years of age."

"That is easy. Paul, will you marry me? Will you be my husband?"

"Yes, sweetheart, I will," answers Paul as he pulls Delilah close and they kiss.

"The only drawback is we can't have a traditional wedding," says Paul.

"What is a traditional wedding?"

"Well, there is a lot to a traditional wedding; white wedding dress, a minister, a church and many invited people."

"Paul, how will we marry?"

"We see the Judge and he will read the vows and we will pledge to each other."

"The Judge is like a Bishop, then?"

"Yes, kind of."

"Paul, I want to wear my Community apparel for the wedding."

"That is fine with me. If there are any other traditions of yours with a marriage, we will see if we can do them."

THE MARRIAGE

"Judge, this is Delilah, of whom I have been courting."

"Hello, Delilah. It is nice to meet you. Why have you come to me?"

"We want to be married…I mean, I want to marry Paul."

"You do realize, Ms. Delilah, your marriage, here, may not be accepted in your Amish Community?"

"Yes, I know, but I love Paul and I want to be married to him in your tradition."

"Paul Matthews, do you take Delilah Ann Yoder to be your lawfully wedded wife in sickness and health; richer or poorer; and vow to protect her until death do you part?"

"I do."

Delilah Ann Yoder, do you take Paul James Matthews to be your lawfully wedded husband in sickness and health; richer or poorer; and vow to cling to him until death do you part?"

"I do."

"Paul, do you have a ring for Mrs. Matthews?" asks Judge Conley.

"Yes, I do."

"Please place the ring on Delilah's finger and repeat after me."

"Delilah, I promise to be at your side and protect you from harm and uphold your womanhood so help me God."

Paul repeats this while slipping the ring on Delilah's finger.

"I pronounce you man and wife; you may kiss the bride," says Judge Conley.

"Paul, what did the Judge mean when he had you repeat what he said placing this beautiful ring on my finger?" asks Delilah.

"Basically, he had me promise I would protect you and uphold my duty to satisfy your needs."

"Satisfy my needs? What does that mean, Paul?"

"It means I remove the *Bundling Board* and never return it to our bed."

"Oh, Paul, I am not sure what my needs are? Can you teach me?"

"Yes, my darling Delilah."

DELILAH'S NEEDS

"*P*aul, your tradition to marry is quite different from marrying in our Community. Once the *bundling board* is removed, do we touch each other? Me being only sixteen years of age, I don't know much about being married to a man and my needs."

"Come here, Delilah and place your arms around my neck. Now allow me to place my hands around your waist. Pull me closer to you and place your lips on mine. Yes, just like that. Now close your eyes and let me kiss you."

"Oh, Paul, I like when you touch my tongue with yours and, oh…"

"What are you feeling Delilah?"

"I am feeling your hands on my rump…"

"What else are you feeling, Delilah?"

"I feel like I want to touch you. I want to touch your chest and I might want to touch your rump, too."

"Go ahead, trust your feelings and do what they are telling you to do," says Paul.

"Paul, I think I need to stop. I don't think what I am feeling is right."

"You are feeling what you should. What you are feeling is your 'needs' Delilah. There is nothing wrong with acting on your feelings. Let us re-visit those feelings later," states Paul.

"Paul, I want to take you to my Community and introduce you to my papa and mama."

"Do you think that is a wise decision, Delilah?"

"Well, maybe in a few days."

JEDEDIAH WARNS DELILAH

"Sis, what is that on your finger?" asks Jedediah.

"I am Mrs. Delilah Matthews."

"Don't tell me you married that Paul, guy?"

"Yes, I did, and I love him so much. I am so happy."

"Delilah, papa will not be happy with what you did in marrying outside the Community. You won't be able to return."

"I don't care, brother. I love Paul."

"You don't even know how to be with a man, sis. Does he know that?"

"Paul is going to teach me. He said I have 'needs' and he is going to show me what my 'needs' are."

"I don't like this, sis. I just don't like it."

DELILAH DISCOVERS HER NEEDS

"*P*aul, I see there is no *bundling board* on the bed," says Delilah.

"Yes, dear, now come over to me. Let me slip your dress off your shoulders."

"But Paul, I don't think..."

"Don't think sweetheart, just let things happen."

"Paul, no man has ever seen me like this."

"Delilah, you are beautiful. Your skin is so soft and the slight crimson glow on your nudity from the sunset, as it peeks through the window curtains, enhances my need to touch and embrace you even more."

"What do I do...?

"Just lie down beside me and let me explore your beauty."

"What do you want me to do, Paul?"

"Just relax and let me place my hands on your thighs. Yes, just like that, now let me push them gently apart."

"Paul, what are you going to do?"

"Relax, Delilah, just let your feelings flow. Do what your feelings are directing."

"Oh, Paul, I feel...I feel so strange down there."

"Go ahead honey, follow your feelings. Now relax…"

"Paul, I feel I am being bad, but I feel like placing my hands on you. I want to…"

"Delilah, do what comes natural…"

"Paul, please move up to my face and kiss me…"

"Let me stop at your breasts…let my tongue dance…"

"Oh, oh, Paul, I feel funny. I am all tingly all over and feel slippery wet down at my bum."

"Now relax darling. I will be gentle. Just let it happen."

"Oh, Paul, oh, what…feels strange…, oh…oh…ahh…oh, yes…"

"Just like that, sweetheart, move your hips rhythmically with me…"

"Oh, Paul, I feel warmth…oh…oh…, I think…I…like it…"

PAUL, COME BACK TO BED

*G*ood morning, sweetheart!"

"Good morning, Paul."

"Did you sleep well, Delilah?"

'Yes, I did, and I felt so protected with your arms around me and your closeness to my body. I dreamt how you made me feel last night."

"Speaking of last night. How do you feel about it?"

"I think I discovered my 'needs' and I think I would like more of it."

"Any time, honey, any time."

"Will you teach me more, Paul?"

"Yes, we have a whole lifetime to learn together."

"Paul come back to bed and hold me. Hold me close and kiss me...."

"You know, dear, this will lead to..."

"I hope so, Paul. I want more of last night..."

MISTER THIMBLE

"Mr. Thimble, I would like you to set up a meeting with Human Resources for me. I need to add my wife to my health insurance."

"So, Paul, does that mean you married that Amish girl? Do you really think that was a wise choice, their Community and all?"

"I love Delilah and I have no problem with marrying an Amish girl."

"Yes, Paul, but she is just a child..."

"Mr. Thimble, will you set that meeting for me?"

"I will, Paul, but I see nothing but problems with your marriage to her."

DELILAH HAS A SECRET

"Delilah, I wish for you to not work so hard in finding employment," states Paul.

"But, Paul, I must earn my keep. It has been over a month now."

"Honey, what would you be doing in your Community once you have become a wife?"

"I would me mending my husband's clothes, tending to the garden, and planning for children."

"There is no need for you to enter into employment. I want you to feel comfortable in doing what your tradition dictates for a married Amish woman."

"But Paul, we have no garden, and we have no children. Your clothes are new and don't need mending."

"Delilah, I wanted it to be a surprise, but I will tell you now. I have purchased a farm not too far from your Community for our home."

"Oh, Paul, you are such a loving husband. Can we have a garden and maybe some milking cows, chickens…"

"We can have whatever you want sweetheart. I want you to be extremely comfortable with life accompanying me as my wife. You will need to mend clothes because I won't need these new clothes once we get to the farm."

"Paul, you will need these clothes for your work, won't you?"

"Yes, but they won't need to be worn as much because I have worked it out with my company to do most of my work at home, on the farm."

"How does that work, Paul?"

"You will see, but there is one more matter we need to discuss."

"Oh, what is it, Paul?"

"Are you willing to start having children, Delilah?"

"Well, er, yes, Paul…I have been meaning to tell you…"

"What honey? Are you….?

"Yes, Paul, I am with child. I am going to give you a child."

"Oh, sweetheart, I am so excited for us! Come here and sit with me."

"Paul, Amish women do not take it easy, especially with child. We work and extremely hard. God watches over us and protects us."

JEDEDIAH IS GOING TO BE AN UNCLE

"Jedediah, you are going to be an uncle," says Delilah excitedly.

"Sis, you didn't! You should have kept the *bundling board* in your bed a while longer."

"Oh, Jedediah, what are you so afraid of?"

"You won't be able to re-join the Community. A husband and now a child, not Amish!"

"I may not want to re-join the Community. Paul and I are going to live on a farm and he has assured me that I can live our tradition even in his tradition."

"When are you going to tell mama and papa what you have done, Delilah?"

"Soon. Me and Paul will be taking a trip out there soon."

"Don't expect acceptance," states Jedediah.

MIND YOUR OWN BUSINESS, LINDA

"*P*aul, I can't believe you actually married that Amish girl, Della is it?"

"Linda, my wife's name is Delilah and what is it you have a problem with my marriage to her?"

"Well, she isn't like us. How are you going to keep her happy? Are you thinking of becoming Amish, Paul?"

"No, Linda, but I am setting up our life to encompass her traditions. I have purchased a farm for us to live and Delilah is going to be doing what Amish woman do when they become a wife."

"Sure, Paul, I am going to have to see how that works out for you."

"It will be just fine, Linda."

"So, have you knocked her up yet, Paul?"

"Linda, my private life with Delilah is just that, so please do not pry!"

BEN BECOMES INTERESTED IN DELILAH

"*P*aul, me and the guys just heard from Linda you got hitched with that Amish child," says Ben.

"Ben, she is not a child; she is my wife and none of your business."

"Oh, come on, Paul, she is only sixteen. I call that rape, don't you?"

"Ben, Amish girls marry at sixteen years of age. It is their tradition."

"Yeah, I suppose you married an Amish child just so you can have sex with a child?"

"Ben, I am warning you. My life with my wife, Delilah, is no business of yours. I don't want to talk about it, and I take offense with your statement, especially from a guy who fucks anything with a dress on."

"Wrong, Paul, I fuck them with their dresses removed."

PAUL TELEMARKETS

"*P*aul please come into my office," states Mr. Thimble.

"What is it you want Mr. Thimble?"

"I am a little concerned. Many of the office personnel are talking about your marriage with that Amish girl."

"Mr. Thimble, I wish you to address my wife by her name, Delilah."

"OK, but your marriage to Delilah has caused much stir within the office."

"You have the authority to stop it, Mr. Thimble!"

"They are speaking such things such as you are a child rapist."

"And you, Mr. Thimble, what do you say?"

"Well, she is quite young and usually one cannot marry a girl of that age unless she is…"

"She is what, Mr. Thimble? Pregnant?"

"Well, I don't mean it that way, Paul."

"Delilah and I married under Amish law and that is all I am going to discuss with you. So, what is it to be, are you asking me to leave my employment with the company?"

"Well, no, but our arrangement for you to work from home will be beneficial to quieting the office stir."

DELILAH ASKS FOR HER
SATISFACTION

"Paul, I want to lie with you now," says Delilah.

"Are you sure it will be OK, honey?"

"I don't believe you can hurt the child, Paul, and I am learning more about my 'needs' very quickly!"

"Here, Paul, wrap your arms around me and unzip my dress. Now, slide around the back of me and place your hands on my thighs; yes, like that. Now slowly slide them up and let your palms feel the contours of my body…"

"Delilah, dear, I thought you didn't know much…?"

"It didn't take long for my mind to get in touch with my 'needs'. Kiss me Paul!"

"I promise I will be careful, sweetheart," says Paul.

"Oh Paul, I love you so much!"

"Are you sure I won't hurt the child?"

"Paul, relax, just follow your feelings, like you have been telling me all along. I will reciprocate."

"Oh, Delilah, my sweetheart…"

"Paul, oh…oh…oh…ahh…more…"

BEN MAKES HIS MOVE

"*H*ello, I will be there in a minute. Oh, hello, you are Ben?" asks Delilah.

"Yes, you are correct, my name is Ben, and I am one of Paul's friends. I assume you are Delilah?"

"Paul is not here now, but I expect him to be back within the hour. I will tell him you stopped by."

"So, how does your marriage to Paul stack up with your Amish tradition?"

"I really don't want to talk about that. I will let Paul know you stopped by."

"Look, Delilah, I am curious just what an Amish girl looks like with her dress off!"

"Ben, I am asking you to leave right now!"

"I am afraid that won't be possible, now take a seat on the couch and let me get to know you better."

"Ben, let go of my arms!"

"If you would just cooperate with me, it will be much easier. Do you Amish girls wear panties? Well, do you? Maybe we shall see!"

"Ben, let go of me! Don't touch my legs!"

"Here, honey, stop resisting and spread those thighs of yours while I take a peek!"

"No, Ben! Please don't do that!"

"Why you Amish girls wear such long dresses. It will take me a lot of time just to get all of this material up to your knees."

PAUL RESCUES DELILAH

"Benjamin! Remove your hands from my wife!"

"Oh, Paul, I am so glad you are here!" exclaims Delilah.

"Ben, what the hell are you doing here?"

"Oh, Paul, she and I were just getting to know each other!"

"Paul, that is not true! I told him you were away, and I would tell you he stopped by, but he would not leave and forced me to the couch and placed his hand between my thighs while pinning my arm and body to the couch. He was trying to lift my dress and spread my legs to see if I had pants on, he called them panties, when you came in!"

"I know, Delilah, I seen and heard all I needed to know what he was trying to do to you. Now get the hell out of here Ben!"

"I need to know, honey, do Amish girls wear panties, er pants under your dresses or is your bare pussy just showing?"

"That's it Ben! Get the hell out of here and if I ever catch you even looking at my wife, I swear I will kill you!"

WHAT ARE PANTIES?

"Thank God, you came home when you did, Paul."

"Delilah, when I am not here, I don't want you to answer the door for anyone."

"What is going on Paul?"

"Some people I know are having issues I married you, an Amish girl, and think I am a cradle robber because of your age."

"What are panties, Paul?"

"They are a type of pants you put on before you put on your outer pants or dress."

"Oh, those black and red colored things that barely cover my bum you bought for me?"

"Yes, how do you like them?"

"I don't wear them all of the time. I do not happen to be wearing them now. They are so constricting."

"It is a good thing I came home when I did. How far did he get your dress up?"

"Just to my knees. I am sure he could not see any of me under there. Thank God I have a long dress on. I still don't understand the women in your tradition wearing those dresses that show their legs to their knees, let alone way above the knees."

"Your clothes are OK with me Delilah. I have no complaints."

"Paul, what is a pussy?"

"It is a slang word for the entrance point on a woman."

"Do you mean…down there? He was trying to see my woman-hood. Only you can see me there!"

"Yes, dear, and he wasn't going to stop there."

"You mean he wanted to 'get connected' with me?"

"Yes, Delilah."

THE BOYS ARE JEALOUS

"*H*ello, Paul. What do you want this late in the evening? Oh, hello…," says Linda.

"My name is Delilah. I am Paul's wife."

"Linda, what the hell have you been telling your 'boys'?"

"What are you talking about, Paul?"

"Ben was at my home this afternoon while I was out and tried to rape Delilah."

"Did he do it?"

"No, I came home just in time to stop it. I do not care about the parties you run here and the things you encourage the guys to do with their dates in your bedrooms, but I am warning you that Delilah is off limits, and I will kill anyone of them who touches her! You better warn all of them, Linda!"

"Paul, I didn't encourage Ben to do that!"

"You may not have directly, but your testosterone boosting parties gives those guys ideas that reach far beyond your bedrooms."

"You do know, Paul, they are jealous of you because you have a very young girl you can bed anytime you want without the law breathing down your throat."

"Linda, my marriage to Delilah was done in the Amish tradition which is acceptable in their laws. Nothing was done illegally."

"Yes, Paul, but…."

"No buts, Linda. It is none of your business and you had better let the guys know the same."

"OK, OK, Paul, don't get so angry."

"Linda, Ben was about to rape my wife; I shouldn't be angry?"

"Paul, are we going to have this kind of trouble now?"

"No, Delilah, we won't have any more trouble. I made my point."

MEETING MAMMA AND PAPA

"*I* think we should go to my Community and tell them the news about us," says Delilah.

"Do you think it is wise?" asks Paul.

"Yes, they need to know what their daughter has been up to. Let us go this weekend."

"Mama, papa?"

"Hello, Delilah. You have decided to come back from the outside world?"

"No, not really, mama."

"And who is this, Delilah?"

"This is Paul, papa."

"Hello, Paul. So why are you visiting us, Paul?"

"Mama, that is why I am here. Paul is my husband."

"Delilah, you are married?"

"Yes, we love each other, papa, and we got married in the Amish tradition."

"The Amish tradition?"

"Yes, mama. In Paul's tradition, he cannot marry a woman of my age, but if I say I want to marry him, we can get married. It does sound strange, but that is how we were able to marry."

"But, Delilah, you married Paul and he isn't from our Community."

"Why should that make a difference, papa?"

"We don't think the elders will allow Paul to be of our Community."

"I wasn't thinking of coming back to the Community, mama."

"Delilah, you should have found a man in our Community to marry."

"But I didn't mama and I love Paul. Isn't that what it is all about? We are going to be living on a farm and I will be tending the cows, mending, sewing, gardening…. just like in our Community."

"Delilah, in our eyes you are not married to this Paul. Have you removed the *bundle board*?"

"Papa, of course. I am married to him."

"In our eyes, Delilah, you have committed fornication. You know Amish women cannot marry outsiders."

"I know, papa, but I am not returning to the Community. I knew you would not accept me!"

"Delilah, if you wish to stay, you will have to publicly abolish your connection with him."

"Mama, I am with child. You will have a grandchild."

"No, Delilah, you are no longer of the Yoder family. Your fornication has given you an illegitimate child."

"Papa, my child is of my marriage. It isn't illegitimate!"

"Delilah, since you have acted out in their marriage ritual and not ours, you have fornicated against your body producing a child, we have no choice but to treat you as an adult, even though you have not been baptized, and you will be shunned. You have no family here and we will not welcome you into our Community!"

"Papa, you can't! Are you sure it is what you want? Mama, please say something that will change papa's feelings."

"Delilah, your father's word is his word and not to be challenged!"

"Go, Delilah! Go now and never return!"

"Oh, papa…"

"Delilah, dear, I am so sorry for you."

"Don't be, Paul. I knew I would be shunned. I love you Paul and nothing will ever change my feelings for you! Let's go live our life at our farm," says Delilah.

JEDEDIAH DENOUNCES DELILAH

"Hey, Jedediah!"

    "I don't know you Delilah."

"So, mama and papa got to you already!"

"Take your stuff out of my apartment and never step foot in here again. I no longer have a sister."

"Jedediah, you don't mean that."

"I do! Hurry up and get your stuff and leave!"

MOVING DAY & COMPROMISING

"*I*t is moving day, Delilah."

"Paul, I have waited so much for this day. I can't wait to get settled in."

"Delilah, what are your ideas for a name for our baby?"

"If it is a boy, I would like the name Levi and if it is a girl, I would like the name Sarah. What do you think, Paul?"

"I like those names very much. By the way, I think we need to get you to a doctor and have a checkup on your pregnancy. You are really starting to show, and we should be sure all things are OK."

"Paul, whatever you feel, but I am going to have our child at home."

"I am OK with that, Delilah, but I am concerned, and I don't know how to deliver a baby."

"God will guide us, Paul.

"OK, dear."

"Paul, I am not used to having a 'say' in anything being an Amish woman. Your tradition is so different than the Amish tradition."

"Sweetheart, in my tradition, the woman has a 'say' and in a marriage the husband and wife work together with compromises. Is this going to be OK with you?"

"What are compromises, Paul?

"Well, everyone has their own way of thinking of things or acting in certain situations…"

"In our Community, Amish woman are not allowed to voice much."

"OK, say I want us to go to the store today at two in the afternoon and you tell me you don't feel like going to the store at that time because you have something else you are doing. An example of a compromise would be like I say to you, OK, we can wait until you are done with what you are doing and then go to the store. You reply that my idea is a good one and that is what we plan."

"Interesting. I have never heard that happening in our Community," says Delilah.

"It is just one example of a compromise. Sometimes compromising is not that simple and it isn't about giving in to your wife or husband but coming to a mutual agreement that fits all circumstances or modifies them to be suitable to each other," says Paul.

"It is fine with me, but you will need to ask for my input often because I am not used to compromises in the Amish Community."

BEN'S CONFESSES TO LINDA

"en, Paul paid me a visit a few weeks ago threatening me to talk to you about the incident with you and his Amish wife," says Linda.

"Yeah? What incident are you talking about?"

"Paul said you entered into his house and was bothering his wife in an inappropriate manner."

"I did pay her a visit. I did not lay a hand on her. All I wanted is for her to show me whether she was wearing panties. I heard Amish girls don't wear any."

"I see, Ben, so you were trying to see if her snatch was bare?"

"Yes, that is all. I wasn't going to do anything to her."

"Paul said you were about to rape her."

"No way! I wouldn't lay a hand on her."

"She is with child now…"

"Yeah, it sure didn't take him long to knock her up!"

"Ben, you and the boys need to leave Paul and his wife alone."

"Linda, I haven't been near them since the incident you talk about."

"You had better not because I don't know what Paul may be capable of. He threatened to kill you if you ever lay a hand on his wife."

"Don't worry Linda, I am not planning on visiting her, especially now that she is knocked up. My intrigue is with a virgin."

"Ben, it has been a few months since Paul married her, do you think they weren't having relations until now?" asks Linda.

"It doesn't matter. I probably would have caught something from her anyhow. I hear those girls are not the cleanest, well, you know, down there."

BEN CONFRONTS JEDEDIAH

"*H*ey you! Aren't you that Amish girl's brother?" asks Ben.

"I don't have any sisters," answers Jedediah.

"Oh, come on, I have seen you with her."

"She is no longer my sister."

"What do you mean, she is no longer your sister?"

"She broke our tradition and married an outsider. That is not recognized by us."

"Oh, is that how it works?" asks Ben.

"She also fornicated with him," says Jedediah.

"You just said she married that guy. What do you mean she fornicated?"

"In my tradition, marrying an outsider is not recognized, therefore she is not married, and she is with child. Having a child without a husband is fornication."

"I see, so what are you and the others going to do about it?" asks Ben.

"It is finished. She is shunned from our Community."

"Shunned?"

"Yes, shunned. She is no longer recognized as part of my family or the Community. She can never return to us," says Jedediah.

WE NEED A MIDWIFE

"*D*elilah, do you think you can get one of the women from your Community to help in birthing our child?" asks Paul.

"No Paul, not one of them will be allowed to help. Remember, I am shunned."

"We need a mid-wife, Delilah."

"I am afraid we are on our own, Paul. I will have our child here and you will be the mid-wife."

"But honey, I have no idea of how to help birthing a child."

"I don't either, Paul, but I have seen it done with other women in our Community. When the time comes, God will give us the strength."

BEN IS OBSESSED WITH DELILAH

"*S*am, what do you think about that Amish girl?" asks Ben.

"You mean the one who Paul supposedly married?"

"Yeah, her. I talked to her brother and he said she isn't married to Paul."

"What do you mean, Ben?"

"He said in his tradition, an Amish girl is not recognized as being married to an outsider. She isn't really married."

"So what, Ben. Who cares?"

"Well, I was hesitant when I invited myself in her home while Paul was out and tried to get her to show me whether she was wearing panties or not, being married. But now, knowing she is not really married, well, I could have gone further."

"Are you talking about having relations with her, Ben?"

"Yeah, I could have fucked her and not felt bad fucking a married woman."

"Ben, just leave it alone…leave her alone. She has Paul and she is fucking him. Wouldn't you rather have a virgin? It is the only thing you preach!" exclaims Sam.

"Yeah, I guess so, but it just ain't fair!"

"What's not fair, Sam?"

"It isn't fair that Paul was able to bed such a young girl who is actually so pretty…"

"Ben, you need to drop the jealousy. It won't get you anywhere."

"It just ain't right, Sam. It just ain't right."

LINDA A MIDWIFE?

"*H*ello, Paul, I didn't expect to ever see you at my doorstep," says Linda.

"Linda, I have a favor to ask you."

"What now, Paul?"

"Well, you being a woman, well, you must know about how women give birth?"

"I do know where babies come from and you must know how your wife got pregnant."

"It is not that, Linda. See, Delilah is going to have the child in a couple of months. She is shunned from her Community due to marrying me and has no chance of having a mid-wife. I know nothing of delivering children and Delilah wants to have her child at home."

"You are in quite a pickle, Paul. Maybe you should have thought about that before you decided to marry her and especially before you knocked her up!" exclaims Linda.

"Linda don't be so crude! Delilah is my wife and within our marriage she is with child."

"So, are you asking that I help Delilah deliver her baby? You want me to be her mid-wife?"

"I was hoping you might know someone who has the ability. I

already know how you feel about Delilah and me, so I wouldn't be asking you," says Paul.

"I don't know anything about popping babies, so you are correct in not thinking I would help. But take this number down and call her. Liz is a young girl who has been a mid-wife for many girls that I know."

"How reliable is she?" asks Paul.

"Well, she is the one who delivers the babies for the girls my boys knock-up."

LIZ

"Hello, is this Liz?" asks Paul.

"Yes, it is," says Liz.

"I understand you have experience in birthing babies."

"Yes, I do. Is it a girl you have been with?" asks Liz.

"No, actually it is my wife."

"So, you aren't one of Linda's boys?"

"No, my wife Delilah Yoder is due to birth our child in a couple of months and she is going to deliver at home."

"What? No hospital? No doctor?"

"She is from the Amish Community and they do not believe in our tradition of childbirth."

"How in the world have you been successful in marrying her?" asks Liz.

"It is a long story, but we are legally married by way of her tradition."

"Her tradition?"

"Yes, you see, she is very young…"

"Oh, I see. She is typical to the ones I have assisted in birthing."

"Does age have anything with the way childbirth happens?" asks Paul.

"No, it is just the younger they are, the easier it is safety-wise, but girls have no clue what the night of fun ends up entailing."

"Liz, she is my wife," says Paul.

"Ok, I will help you out. Give me a call a week before she is due. I will need a place to stay until she delivers," says Liz.

"That will be no problem. We have plenty of rooms for you to stay in. Thank you, Liz is it?"

"Yes, and you are?"

"Oh, I am sorry, my name is Paul, Paul Yoder."

"She wanted to keep her maiden name?"

"Yes."

BEN HAS ILL INTENTIONS

"*R*andy, what do you think about Paul and that Amish girl he calls his wife?" asks Ben.

"Oh, I don't know, I haven't thought about it. What is on your mind, Ben?"

"Well, don't you think Paul has robbed the cradle with such a young girl?"

"I think he is lucky."

"Yeah, but it isn't fair he has such a beauty, and he has already knocked her up."

"I didn't think your aim was to knock-up your girls, Ben?"

"It isn't, but he is lucky to have her all to his own. Can you imagine having her all to your own to fuck whenever you want, Randy?"

"You can have the same thing, Ben, if only the girls you fucked would marry you!"

"It just ain't fair!"

"Ben, are you jealous of Paul?"

"No! I wanted her before Paul got his hands on her."

"Oh, you mean at the party that night? You would have never scored with her. Paul had her under his guard all the time they were there."

"Randy, I will have my chance with her someday!"

"Ben, come on, how do you plan on that? Why don't you just drop it and find another girl. She isn't the only pretty girl."

"Yeah, but her being Amish and all….it is intriguing," says Ben.

"Amish or not, Ben, they all fuck the same!" exclaims Randy.

LIZ IS THE MIDWIFE

"Hello, is this Liz?"

"Yes."

"This is Paul Yoder. My wife, Delilah is a week away from her birthing."

"How do you know that? Has she been to a doctor?" asks Liz.

"No, she says she just knows."

"Ok, but if she is incorrect, it will cost you more."

"That is OK, I trust she knows."

LINDA'S PARTY

"Linda, I hear you are having another party next week?" asks Sam.

"Yes, and it will be an 'all out' party! Make sure you tell the other boys. Encourage them to bring more than one girl with them. There will be plenty of opportunities for all of them to get 'laid'."

"You mean you will allow us to have more than one girl that night?"

"Yup! It is my once a year treat for you boys," says Linda.

LISTEN TO THE BABY

"*D*elilah, dear, let me hear our little one," says Paul.

"Paul put you ear right here over my navel. The child's head is in that area at this time," says Delilah.

"I think I hear her talking."

"Paul, how do you know the child is a girl?"

"It has to be. She will be as beautiful as her mama."

"Oh, Paul, I need to give you a boy to withhold the family name."

"We will get the boy after she comes into the world."

"We will just have to start working on that in time," says Delilah.

"A very short time, sweetheart!" says Paul.

PAUL IS OUT OF TOWN

"*D*elilah, the boss wants me to meet with the staff this weekend. It will only be for a couple days."

"I hope I don't have our child then," says Delilah.

"Luckily, we have your mid-wife."

"Paul, I will call you if I am about to birth. I want you to be here."

"Honey call before that. I wouldn't miss it for a minute."

"Liz, I will be out of town for the next couple of days. Please call me if Delilah is about to birth," says Paul.

"If I call, you had better be on your way. She is young and I expect her to take some time popping out the child, but one never knows. Has she had any children before this one?"

"No, this is her first child."

"It will take time, but you get here as fast as you can," says Liz.

GIRLS, GIRLS, GIRLS

"*L*inda, this is a hell of a party! Where is Ben, Randy and Sam?" asks George.

"Upstairs. They have already started," says Linda.

"Well, this here is Lucy, and this is Lizzy," says Ted.

"This is Belinda and Sarah," says George.

"Great! Get them some drinks. Loosen them up some," says Linda.

"Don't worry Linda, they know what they are her for," says Ted.

"Hey, Ben, good to see you! I see you have your fill of girls," says Randy.

"Hell, yeah. These sluts have tight pussies," says Ben.

"Well, here are some to be broken in. Do you think you can do that, Ben?" asks Ted.

"The more the merrier! Come with me girls!"

"Ben, before you fuck them, tell me where your buddy Jimmy is? He never misses this party," says Randy.

"I don't know, but I expect he will be here later," says Ben.

"Well, I hope he has something left when he gets here. These girls are looking for a wild ride!" exclaims Randy.

DELILAH WILL DIE?

"*D*elilah how are you feeling?" asks Liz.

"I am doing OK, but I feel those pains more often."

"We don't have to worry until your water breaks," says Liz.

"What is the water?" asks Delilah.

"Girl, you don't know much about birthing babies, do you? The water is the fluid your baby is floating in. It must come out of you before you birth the baby. That is when we know you will have the baby soon."

"Liz, I think there is someone at the door. Please close this door before you answer the knock. I don't want anyone seeing me here."

"Hello, who are you? Hey, get your hands off me!"

"Shut up you Amish slut!"

"Who the hell are you?' asks Liz.

"Let's just say I am your savior!"

"Savior?"

"Yeah, if I don't do what I came here for, you will be fucked so much you won't be able to walk!"

"Listen!"

"Shut the fuck up bitch!"

"Where are you taking me to?"

"Just get in there and strip off your clothes!"

"No…"

"Get in the bathtub and place your legs up on the rim!"

"What are you going to do?"

"Lay still! I suggest you arouse yourself; it will not hurt so much. Now get to it! You know how to do it! Keep it going. I will help you. I will just sit back here and massage your head; run my fingers through your hair. You are doing a great job. I do not care if you moan, scream, whimper, or whatever it is you do when you arouse yourself. Keep it going…yes, that is it! Are you going to "cum" bitch?"

"Yes…oh, why are you making me do this…oh…ahhhh…"

"Keep it up bitch!"

"Ah…oh…is this what you want?"

"It is amazing what I can make you do as long as I have this knife at your neck."

"When this is all over, what will you do………?" questions Liz as she slowly drifts into unconsciousness.

"It is done Bitch! You see, I had to kill you! If I cannot have you, then no one will! You see, in having you in the bathtub, the slit in your throat won't make a mess on the floor."

DELILAH'S DISCOVERY

"*L*iz, Liz? Are you OK? Who was it? Are you OK? I heard some scuffling and voices. You were moaning, I think," says Delilah.

"Ah…. he…l…p…." says Liz in her last breath.

"Liz, where are you? Liz? OH MY GOD! LIZ, OH LIZ…! Screams Delilah as she opens the bathroom door.

"Paul, Paul, you need to get here!" exclaims Delilah as soon as she places the call.

"What is it sweetheart? Are you having the child? Where is Liz?"

"Paul, I…I…Liz…is…get here, oh, my water just broke! Paul, get here now!

SHE WAS SUPPOSED TO HAVE A BABY?

"Hey, Jimmy, nice to see you. I was beginning to think you weren't going to show," says Linda.

"I am here. Where is Ben?"

"He is upstairs. I believe he is in the middle of bedding down at least two of those girls," says Linda.

"I need to see him right away!"

"Go on up. He might let you take part."

"Hey, Ben, you in there?" asks Jimmy.

"Jimmy, is that you? Hang on, I will be out in a minute," says Ben.

"What the hell you got going on in there, Ben?"

"Jimmy, I have two butt naked girls in there, in my bed with their legs spread apart. They are waiting for me; now did you get it done?"

"Yes, I did! Did you make sure to kill the baby too?"

"Baby? What baby?"

DELILAH AND BABY ARE SAFE

"*D*elilah are you OK?" asks Paul.

"Paul, come in the bedroom and see your daughter."

"You had the child? What? Where is Liz?"

"Paul, don't go into the bathroom."

"Why, honey?"

"Paul hold her. Isn't she so beautiful?"

"Yes Delilah, she is as beautiful as her mama."

"Paul, I birthed her all by myself."

"What about Liz? She didn't help you?"

"Paul, don't go into the bathroom."

"Delilah, what is the matter? Why do you keep saying that?"

"Paul, don't..."

"Here, sweetheart, she is hungry. Put her to your breast. "Mama and our daughter, so sweet," says Paul.

CONFUSION OF PLANS

"What the hell do you mean by 'what baby'?" asks Ben.

"Hey boy, are you going to just let us dry up on you? We are waiting for that big boy!"

"I will be in shortly, just keep those juices running...you know how to do it!" exclaims Ben.

"The Amish girl was with child, Jimmy. If you got the job done, who in the hell did you do it to?" asks Ben.

"She wasn't pregnant, Ben."

'Was there anyone else in there?"

"No, she was all alone. I dragged her to the bathtub naked just like you told me to do. I made her arouse herself...kind of what I wanted her to do, and just as she was to "cum", I slit her throat."

"Jimmy, you killed the wrong woman! Who was the woman you killed?"

"I don't know. You didn't tell me she was pregnant!"

SO WHAT HAPPENED?

"What the hell happened in here, Delilah?" screams Paul. "I told you to not go into the bathroom."

"Delilah,…what happened?"

"Paul, I don't know. Someone knocked on the door and I told Liz to close me in the bedroom. I heard some scuffling and them she moaned and whimpered. I was afraid, so I did not say anything or even move. When I heard the door close, I called for Liz and she did not respond. I went into the bathroom and, well, you see…she was alive enough to call for help and then she was gone. I called you and my water broke. I am sorry, I made a mess."

"Don't worry about that honey."

"I felt the child coming, so I went over there in the corner and squatted down. I pushed and I pushed and out she came. I had seen in our Community the midwife clamp off the tube from me to her and I found a clothes pin and then I cut it with a kitchen knife. I then pushed it in, so her belly button looked like other children's. I made a mess, and I was so mesmerized, I did not have the strength to clean it up. Hold her and I will clean up my mess."

"Sit tight, dear, let her suckle. I will clean up."

"Oh, Paul, I love you so much. I don't know what I would have done if you hadn't come to me."

THIS TIME DO IT CORRECTLY

"Jimmy, you need to be careful. Are you sure she didn't recognize you or you left something there?"

"She was practically dead when I left, and I didn't leave anything. I even have the knife I used. Besides, I am not taking the rap for this. You had me do this!"

"Nobody is going to get in trouble. She is dead and cannot identify you and there are no clues, so do not worry. You do need to get to the Amish girl."

"No, no, Ben. I am through! You will have to do that yourself!"

LIZ IS DEAD, LINDA

"*L*inda, we have a problem!"

"Hello, Paul. I am beginning to think you like talking to me."

"Linda, something has happened to Liz."

"Oh, did she take the job in birthing your child?"

"Linda, she is dead!"

"What the hell are you saying, Paul?'

"She was at my house when Delilah was ready to birth our daughter."

"Oh, congratulations to having a daughter."

"Someone came into our home and murdered Liz in the bathroom. They slit her throat while she was lying in the bathtub."

"Does anyone know who might have done it and why?" asks Linda.

"No, but my guess is that someone mistook Liz for my Delilah."

"What makes you think that Paul?"

"There are some people in this community that are not fond of my marriage to an Amish girl."

"Do you really think someone would want to kill your wife because of that?" asks Linda.

"Well, that Ben of yours tried to rape her," states Paul.

"Ben is not mine. He is just a customer."

"The police will be asking questions and I am sure they will be questioning all of the boys who frequent your parties," says Paul.

LINDA QUESTIONS BEN

"*B*en, come over here," says Linda.

"What do you want, now?"

"Ben, do you remember the girl who acts as the mid-wife to the girls you boys knock-up?"

"None of the girls I have fucked are knocked-up!"

"None that you know of..."

"What's her name...Liz, I think," says Ben.

"Yes, Liz. She was found in the home of Paul and his Amish wife, dead."

"Dead? What the hell for?"

"Paul believes whoever did it was mistaken that Liz was the Amish girl."

"Why would that be, Linda? Why would anyone want to kill Liz or that Amish girl?"

"As I recall, Ben, you have been quite jealous of Paul for marrying that Amish girl."

"I got over that, Linda."

"Did you, Ben? You almost raped her?"

"Linda, you are not going to pin that on me. I was here at the party all night and you know it!"

"Ben, I didn't say when this happened," says Linda.

NO BOTTLE FOR SARAH

"Delilah, how is Sarah?"

"She is sleeping now. I hope she sleeps for a while. I am getting very tired and she always wants me in the middle of the night."

"Do you think we should give her a bottle?"

"No, Paul, our babies are going to come to breast for their hunger. I just need to take a little rest."

"OK, dear. I have to go and meet one of those boys of Linda's."

"Oh, what for?"

"I don't know, but Linda told me that one of them wants to talk to me about something."

"Be careful, Paul. Those boys are up to no good, you know."

RANDY SPILLS IT

"*H*ello, Paul is it?"

"Yes, my name is Paul, and you are?"

"My name is Randy and I want to talk to you about something."

"Sure, sit down here, Randy."

"Paul or Mr. Yoder..."

"You can call me Paul."

"Paul, a friend of mine, Ben..."

"Oh, him! You do know he tried to take advantage of my wife, Delilah?"

"Yes, I heard him brag about it. I am sorry that he did what he did to her."

"Oh, what did he say he did to her?"

"He said he lifted her dress and noticed, well, he said he was able to enter her."

"He is a liar, Randy. He never laid a hand on her in that way. I was there at the time he was about to lift her dress and he didn't do anything such as he brags."

"Paul, he is very jealous of you."

"Jealous?"

"Yes. He is jealous because you have such a young wife all to yourself who you can, well, you know, fuck, anytime you want."

"Randy, I am married to her and it is none of anyone's business what goes on in our marriage."

"I am sure, Paul, but I think his jealousy has gotten so bad that he may do harm to you or your wife. I think he feels that if he can't have your wife, then no one can, especially you."

"Where is Ben now? Did you lure me out here so Ben could get to my wife?"

"No, Paul. I am not here because of that. He is at Linda's when I left, and he had some girls with him. I am sure he is not going to your wife."

THE SLUT

"Delilah, sorry to have awoken you from your nap," says Paul.

"It is OK, Paul. Sarah decided to get hungry, so you know what that means."

"Don't question me, dear, but make sure the door is locked and let no one in. I am on my way back to you."

"Ok, Paul."

"I am going out, Linda."

"Where are you going Ben?"

"Just out."

"What the hell is the matter with that guy? He barely pulled out and then he just leaves," says Judy.

"Judy, what did you expect? Don't you come here for a quick fuck?" says Linda.

"Well, he could have at least fingered my clit!"

"Go wash up, Judy! His cum is running down your legs," says Linda.

"Damit! He said he was wearing a rubber! That bastard might have knocked me up!"

"Play with fire girl…"

BEN ASSAULTS DELILAH AGAIN

"Who is there?" yells Delilah.

"Open the door. This is the police. We heard there might be someone in danger here," says Ben.

"I am O.K."

"Please open the door, ma 'am."

"No, I can't do that. Please go away. I am all right. There is no danger here," says Delilah.

"You need to open the door, miss!" exclaims Ben.

"What…what are you doing? You shouldn't…," exclaims Delilah.

"Don't you know police can pick locks?"

"You…you…you aren't the police. You are that guy Ben."

"That is right, sweetheart. I am here to finish what I came to do earlier. Remember where we left off? You were going to show me whether you have panties on or not," states Ben.

"Listen. I am with child," says Delilah.

"Yeah, I know. Your man Paul knocked you up!"

"I have a child to feed…"

"So what! Is it sleeping? I will be incredibly quiet, but you need to muffle your moans."

"I told you. I am with child!"

"You mean Paul knocked you up again? Lucky guy."

"Listen, please leave. Paul will be here any minute," states Delilah.

"Yeah, that is what you said before."

"I was right, wasn't I?"

"I will be gentle, I promise. I will not hurt your baby. I heard women can fuck even if they are knocked up, even if they have the so-called baby bump. Now, I do not want to hurt you. Just move over there on the couch and lay down on your stomach," says Ben.

"No, I..."

"Please, do it. Do I need to place you there?"

"No, no, please don't touch me! Please leave...All right, all right, I am going."

"If you would just cooperate. Now, do you have panties on? O.K., I will just see for myself.... awe, ouch ahhh...," Ben whimpers as he rolls off Delilah and onto the floor.

JEDEDIAH SAVES HIS SISTER

"Here, let me fix your dress. Now easy. I will help you up."

"Who, who are you?" asks Delilah.

"Delilah..."

Jedediah, what? What are you doing here? I thought..."

"Sis, I came here to tell you papa has passed on, and then I walked in on this. Are you O.K.? Did he touch you...?

"No, no. You came in the nick of time. What did you do to him?"

"Well, sis, the only thing I could do. He won't bother you again."

"Delilah? Jed..."

"Jedediah, Paul," responds Jedediah.

"Yes. What is going on here? Is that Ben on the floor? Oh, and what happened?"

"Paul, dear, Ben broke through the lock saying he was the police. He forced me on the couch. Then my brother showed up and well, you see what happened," says Delilah.

"Honey, did he hurt you?"

"No, Paul, I am O.K."

"We will need to call the police," says Paul.

"Sis, like I said, Papa is no longer with us. Mama would like you to come to the Community," says Jedediah.

"I thought I was shunned," states Delilah.

"Mama wants you to come."

"I will only come if Sarah can come with me...and Paul."

"Mama says it is O.K."

"Paul, dear, can we go now?"

"Yes, dear, as soon as we are finished with the police.

THE SLUT IS BACK

"**J**udy, why are you back here?" asks Linda.

"I was hoping to see Ben so he can finish what he started."

"You girls never learn. I haven't seen Ben since last night when he left here."

"You mean when he left me dripping with his load?"

"Judy, just go back home. Forget about Ben. He does not care about you or any other girl he beds down. All he wants is a place to unload his frustrations."

"Oh, you call that stuff frustrations?" asks Judy.

PAPA

"Mama, Papa is gone?"

"Yes, my daughter. He is at peace now."

"But mama…"

"Hush Delilah. Bring my granddaughter here. What did you name her?"

"Her name is Sarah. This is my husband, Paul."

"Yes, I remember you, Paul. Do you love my Delilah?"

"Yes, ma'am, very dearly. I take good care of her."

"I want you to know, Delilah, your papa didn't want to face the fact that you married outside our Community. He couldn't realize that this could happen when you went out into the world outside our Community."

"Mama, I am sure he meant well. Papa was a proud man and followed our traditions with his whole heart," says Delilah.

"Delilah, I want you and Paul to be part of our Community, and of course Sarah too."

"But, mama, we have a farm outside the Community and wish to live our life there and raise our children there."

"That is O.K. dear. I want you to feel welcome into our Community for a visit at any time. The rest of the Community is looking forward to your visits."

I AM WITH CHILD

"*D*elilah, Paul and little Sarah! How have you been? It has been…"

"I know mama, it has been at least a couple of months since we visited last. Paul and I have been so busy with the farm, and little Sarah."

'Little Sarah is growing so fast," says mama Yoder.

"Mama, I have a surprise for you, and you also, Paul."

"What is it Delilah," asks Paul.

"Mama, you will have another grandchild soon. I am with child!"

"Oh, sweetheart, such great news!" exclaims Paul.

"Paul?"

"Yes, Mrs. Yoder."

"I hope you give Delilah many children."

"That shouldn't be a problem, right Delilah?"

"Yes, Paul dear, you are in charge of that."

"Paul, now that we have been invited into the Community, I would like my child delivered there with the midwives," says Delilah.

"O.K. sweetheart, but what about your doctor?"

"We have a doctor in the Community."

"Whatever you want dear," says Paul as he kisses Delilah with a passionate kiss.

"Oh, Paul, please don't ever stop loving me and kissing me and giving me children."

"Never, sweetheart. I love you so much. Come over here and let me place my arms around you…"

"Oh, Paul, you can't give me a child when I am with child."

"That doesn't mean we can't practice for the next one, now does it?

"Paul, I was hoping to bed with you before the night is over."

NINE MONTHS HAS ARRIVED

"Paul, what shall we name her?" asks Delilah.

"How about, Ruth, honey? Wait, what if it is a boy?"

"I feel strongly it is another girl, Paul."

"OK, how about we name her Ruth."

"That name will be perfect, Paul."

"Paul, the doctor does not want us to try for another child, now that we have Ruth, until he feels it is safe," states Delilah.

"Safe? What does he mean by that? You had a natural birth for Ruth with no difficulties?"

"No difficulties that we know of. As a matter of fact, Ruth birthed very quickly."

DELILAH'S DOCTOR VISIT

"*D*elilah, how are you feeling? Are you able to get Ruth to breast?" asks the doctor.

"Yes doctor. I am feeling fine as much as a woman should with two children at her breast. I seem to have enough milk for both. It is surprising that they both want to go to breast at the same time. Sarah is starting to teeth and that can be uncomfortable sometimes."

"There is a trick the midwives will show you to teach them to suckle without pinching the nipple with the teeth."

"Thank the good Lord for that, doctor."

"Delilah, about birthing more babies. I told you that you need to stop trying for a while."

"Yes, Paul is wondering why that is. He is eager to have me with child soon."

"Delilah, I am concerned for your health. You may need to wait more time before being with child again. Stretch out the time."

"Why, doctor? Why?"

"Delilah, I have found an anomaly in your blood that disturbs me. I am not sure what it is, but I am thinking you need to be careful until I find more information."

"But, doctor, Paul and I cannot put the *bundling board* back in our bed. We are so much in love and we need the closeness of possibly leading to be with child. Even if we were to place the *bundling board*, it would not stop us. We will definitely find a way."

"Delilah, I know we don't believe in what they call contraception, but in your case, you just may need to for your health."

"Doctor, the only contraception is abstinence. I don't think we can do it!"

PAUL, DON'T IMPREGNATE DELILAH

"*D*elilah, would it be all right with you if I talk to Paul alone?"

"Yes, I suppose that would be O.K., but Paul and I don't keep secrets and we always work together."

"Delilah, remember, Paul, your husband, is responsible for giving you children. It is his responsibility."

"Yes, doctor, I understand."

"Paul, I have spoken to your wife Delilah about bearing more children. I explained to her I was concerned for her health."

"Yes, she told me what you told her. I don't think we can abstain from our intimacy."

"Paul, I realize that, and Delilah was very adamant she does not want to stop servicing your needs. I have a possible solution for you."

"Anything, doctor. I love Delilah and quite frankly I cannot keep my hands off her. We enjoy each other immensely."

"I understand Paul. This is what I suggest. It is not a sure method but reduces the odds of giving Delilah a child. You should know when you are about to release into her?"

"Yes, very much so."

"As soon as you start to get that feeling, you need pull yourself out of her and release away from her. You need to be sure to remove yourself from her very quickly."

"Doctor, in our tradition, we are able to have the wife give us relief without entering her. Would that be O.K. as long as I can satisfy her manually?"

"Paul, our belief is the only way to release yourself is by the natural movement within her. You will be doing that. It is not against our custom to release outside of her. Besides the *bundling board* and abstinence, this solution is another possible solution to contraception especially for health reasons."

THE DOCTOR'S SOLUTION

"Paul, what did the doctor discuss with you?"

"Honey, he told me about a solution to contraception."

"I hope it doesn't mean we can't try for a child," says Delilah with anticipation.

"Honey, he said that when we are cleaving to each other and when I feel release to pull myself out from you and release outside and away from you."

"Paul, I don't know if that will work for us. Your release is what I wait for. Like I have told you many times, I can feel the swelling of you and the pressure of your release, and the warmth. That process gives me the pleasure of...of..."

"We call it the climax, sweetheart."

"Yes, Paul, I feel all tingly throughout my entire body and I throb. That is my climax, that is my ecstasy!"

"Delilah, dear, when did you learn about the word ecstasy?"

"The good Lord put it in my vocabulary because He knows the pleasure I desire, and it is good."

"Did the doctor say what he felt was the problem with me bearing more children?"

"No, Delilah, he did not."

"Paul, I want to bear a son for you. I want you to be able to have your heritage passed down and carry your Christian name."

"But, dear, we agreed to use your family name as the children's Christian name."

"Paul, our son has to carry your Christian name first and the family name after."

"Delilah, can we try the solution the doctor has suggested, and I believe I can give you the ecstasy you desire."

"How is that Paul?"

"Would you like to test it out now?"

"Sure, I have been waiting for your invitation."

"Oh Paul, honey, I love that feeling…the swelling inside…"

"Delilah, move your legs a little wider while I…"

"Oh, Paul, what are you doing…oh…oh…ahh…ahh…it feels…it feels…oh…ohhhhhhh…I can't stand it…oh…oh… I am throbbing down there! That was pure ecstasy! What did you do?"

"Delilah, no one told you about that area down there?"

"No Paul. Being sixteen, I do not think they thought they needed to. Probably if I had married in our Community, they would have told me."

"Well, sweetheart that area is an erogenous area and when touched or massaged, it will give a similar feeling that I have when I release."

"Do you think it is why I feel ecstasy when we cleave not using the doctor's solution?"

"Definitely, sweetheart."

"Well Paul, my darling, no matter what method we are using, It is beautiful and satisfying for me."

"Did the doctor say how long we have to do 'his solution'?" It has been a couple of months and I feel fine. I do tire sometimes, but that should be normal for a mother of two children still suckling the breast.

"Delilah, I am concerned for your health even though we don't know what the doctor is talking about. The last thing I want is to endanger you in any way."

O.K. Paul, but I miss the cleaving we had before the 'doctor's solution'."

TIME HAS PASSED AND RUTH IS STARTING TO WALK

"*S*arah, please take your sister Ruth out to the barn and feed the chickens. Make sure you show her how to feed them and once you are done with that let her pet the kittens, but not before. You know when she sees those kittens, it is all she is interested in."

"Yes, mama, I will. After that is done, can we help papa with milking the cows?"

"After that, I want you two to come here and help your mama bake cookies and pies. We need fresh bake goods for our booth at the side of the roadway. There are quite a few neighbors who depend upon our bake goods," says Delilah.

"Mama, can we help you in the booth, today?"

"We will see, Sarah, as long as you two finish your chores for today, and yes, you can put the frosting on the cookies as long as you leave some frosting for the cookies and not your mouth," says Delilah with a loving smile.

DELILAH IS OVULATING

"*P*aul, honey! Are you about finished with the repair of those rocking chairs?"

"Yes, sweetheart, give me a few more minutes and I will be done so I can deliver them tomorrow."

"Paul, dear, I know it has been a long day for you, but it is time for us to cleave. I am a little tired myself, but I really need you now."

"Well, with an invitation like that, how can I resist!"

"I want you to know how easy it will be for you. I am not wearing those, what you call panties. You just need to lift my dress and there you are. Oh, Ruth is starting to get teeth, so my nipples are a little tender. Once I am aroused, it shouldn't be a problem."

"I will be careful my dear, but they are part of the foreplay, you know."

"Oh Paul, kiss me and hold me tight. I feel you are ready…push my legs a little wider…yes…yes, slowly…ohh…oh…"

"Delilah honey, please let go of my hips. I feel the pressure…"

"Paul, I feel the pressure and the enlargement…"

"Delilah, let go of my hips so I can pull out….you must…the pressure…ohh…ohh…ohh…I can't pull out…I can't…oh……oh…the release…"

"Honey, the warmth, the enlargement, the throbbing, the ecstasy…"

"Sweetheart, I didn't pull out."

"I know Paul. I did not want you to pull out. It is time for a child… it is time for your son."

"Delilah, my sweetheart, why did you hold me from pulling out from you? I couldn't hold my release!"

"Paul, it is time, I am taking the gamble for conceiving a child. I want to give you a son. I feel fine. This is the time of the month."

"You are ovulating, Delilah?"

"Yes, and I promise you I am now with child."

DOCTOR, I AM WITH CHILD

"Doctor, why did you want to see me?" asks Delilah.

"Well Delilah, I have news for you about your condition. I had to consult with a specialist outside our Community."

"Doctor, I feel fine. I get a little more tired lately. Those girls of ours keep me busy."

"Delilah, the news I have for you worries me."

"Why doctor?"

"It appears you have a blood disorder that originates from your bones. Your body is making more than normal white blood cells. One of the early side effects is tiring easily."

"What does this mean?"

"Delilah, if I can't get your blood disorder under control, you just might only have months…"

"Months, doctor? Months for what?"

"I am sorry Delilah. Months to live."

"Doctor, it can't be! I feel fine! What woman with two children, one still taking breast and the other one questioning everything doesn't feel tired at times?"

"Delilah, I cautioned you being with child. Your body, at this rate, cannot take the trauma. It could shorten your life even more."

"Doctor, I won't accept this!" Delilah responds with tears in her eyes.

"I am sorry Delilah. We need to discuss how I can help you with this in the most comfortable way. There will be a time when you will be in much pain."

"Doctor, my baby…"

"Delilah, are you telling me you are with child?"

"Yes doctor. I would not let Paul pull out. I just wanted to give him a son."

"Delilah, I am afraid you are going to have great difficulty carrying your child, let alone delivering the child alive. It will most definitely kill you."

"No doctor! I will not accept it! I am nineteen years of age, and I am too young to die! I will not accept it! What will Paul do? What will my children do without a mama?" Delilah starts to wail.

"I am sorry Delilah. I wish I had better news for you. Currently the blood disorder you have has no known cure. All I can do is make your life as painless as possible while I can."

"How long, doctor?"

"It is hard to tell, but my guess will be twelve months, but with child, you may die in childbirth if not before."

DELILAH IS IN DENIAL

"*P*aul, I went and seen the doctor today."

"Why Delilah? Does he have more information about your condition? Wait a minute, have you been crying sweetheart?"

"Yes! I went there to tell him I am with child…"

"Delilah, honey, I am so happy! Are you sure?"

"Yes, dear and I feel our child is a boy this time."

"But why the tears?"

"Paul, I am so happy. I cried all the way home from the doctor's office. It is almost like the buggy horses knew about the news. They trotted so proudly bringing me home."

"Delilah, what did the doctor say about you being with child? He warned us."

"I told him it was my doing because I wouldn't let you pull out before your release. Paul, I will remember that moment for the rest of my life. I just knew when I felt you swell and then the warmth of your release inside me, I would be with child and birth a son for you."

"But the doctor wasn't concerned?"

"Oh, he was, but he said that I should be all right if I be careful and get rest. In a little while I will go tell the news to mama Yoder," says Delilah.

~

"Mama Yoder, I have good news for you. I am with child and I am going to birth a son."

"Delilah, how do you know it will be a boy?"

"Mama, I just know just by the way I received Paul."

REBECCA IS SELECTED MIDWIFE

"*D*elilah, my name is Rebecca and I have been selected by the Community to be your mid-wife. How are you feeling?"

"Hi, Rebecca. I am feeling a little tired today and I am growing much bigger than I did with each of the two girls."

"Here, let me look at your belly. Interesting," says Rebecca as she places her ear on Delilah's enlarged womb.

"What is it Rebecca?"

"How many months, Delilah? Three, four?"

"Oh no, Rebecca, I am only two months along. Oh, I am so tired."

"Your belly is the size of a pregnancy much further along and I think I hear something strange."

"Oh? What do you hear?"

"Delilah, I believe you have two babies in there!"

"What? Oh, my! Two sons for Paul?"

"Delilah, how can you be sure your baby or babies are boys?"

"I just know it; I could tell as soon as Paul released into me. It felt so much different that when his release gave us our daughters. Rebecca, do you mind if I lay here for a while? I am so tired. This large belly of mine tires me out."

"Sure, Delilah, take all the time you like. I will be in the other room if you should need me."

MAMA YODER QUESTIONS PAUL

"Mrs. Yoder?"

"Hello Paul. What brings you here?"

"I am looking for my wife Delilah."

"She hasn't arrived at your house? She left here a couple of hours ago. She told me you are going to have a son?"

"No, and I am worried about her. She is tiring more often lately."

"Paul let me tell you a little secret about my daughter, your wife. In case you did not notice, she is carrying your child quite low. Her belly is exceptionally large and must be quite a weight on her body. You can imagine she tires quickly lugging that belly around. I swear she has more than one child there. She is so big."

"She didn't say whether she was to stop somewhere on her way home?" asks Paul.

"The Community has selected the midwife for her. Possibly she went and visited her."

"Mrs. Yoder, where can I find the midwife?"

"Her name is Rebecca, and her home is two houses down the pathway."

"Thank you, Mrs. Yoder."

"Paul, can I ask you a question?"

"Sure, what is it?"

"Do you love my daughter? Are you taking care of her?"

"Mrs. Yoder, I love Delilah so much and she is my life. I do not know what I would do without her. I take care of her; she is so precious and is the most perfect woman; the mother of my children."

"Hello, are you Ms. Delilah's husband?"

"Yes, and you are Rebecca, Delilah's midwife?"

"Yes."

"Where is she? Is she all right?"

"Oh, yes, she is in the other room. She had become very tired. She has been asleep for over an hour."

DELILAH STRUGGLES WITH HER DENIAL

"elilah, honey, are you O.K? I have been worried about you when you hadn't come home."

"Oh, Paul, I am sorry. After breaking the news to mama, I came here to meet Rebecca, my midwife. Suddenly, I became quite tired. I just dosed off for a few minutes."

"Sweetheart, you have been asleep for over an hour. Are you sure you are O.K? Maybe we should visit the doctor while we are here in the Community."

"Paul, I am O.K. Rebecca said she heard what she thinks is two baby boys in my tummy."

"Twins, Delilah? Oh, I am so excited for us!"

"I am pretty tired Paul, and if there are two boys I am carrying, then you might guess why I am so tired?"

"Sweetheart let me help you to the carriage. We will go home, and you can rest some more. I will make for you a glass of warm milk and heat your favorite blueberry muffins."

"Oh, Paul, I love you so much…I am going to miss…,I mean I don't know what I would do without you."

"Delilah dear, I am never going to be far from your side. I love you more than ever. You are my sunshine, and you compete my life. If it were not for that big belly of yours, I would take you to bed right now and spread my love to you!"

"Oh, Paul, let me rest a bit. Afterwards we shall cleave, even with this big belly of mine. You cannot hurt the boys or me. I do need you Paul! I need you badly!"

UNUSUAL CRAVINGS

"Paul, it is almost dawn and I feel full of energy. Thank you for last night. I was sure we could cleave with the condition I am in. I have a craving Paul."

"A craving? In our society, women sometimes crave pickles or ice cream, or something like that when they are with child."

"Paul, dear, nothing like that. I need you; I need you every day!"

"Sweetheart, you have me every day and every night; you have me at all times!"

"No, Paul, not like that. I know I have you at all times. What I mean is that I want us to cleave everyday now. I need your release. Is that possible?"

"Yes, Delilah, but aren't you concerned I will hurt you or the babies?"

"Paul, you can't hurt us. I need your closeness more than ever, currently. I want to be with you; I want to cleave; I need to cleave! Please Paul?"

"Delilah, you know I would never pass up the opportunity for us to cleave. Of course, we can cleave daily if that is what you need!"

"Paul, will you get the girls started this morning? I am a little tired now. Let them know I will tend to them a little later. Let them know I will help them feed the chickens and I will take them in the buggy to see their grand-mama. I want to spend quality time with them today."

"Sure thing honey," says Paul.

PAPA IS MAMMA THIS MORNING

"Papa, where is mama this morning? She always gets us up and helps us get dressed for the day."

"Sarah, mama is resting right now. She is going to help you feed the chickens a little later and take you to visit your grand-mama," responds Paul.

"Papa, why is mama's belly so big?"

"Ruth, your mama is going to have a baby. There is a baby in her tummy. You were there too, before you came into our lives and your sister Sarah."

"Ruth, I will tell you about it later," remarks Sarah.

"You girls are so lucky!"

"Why is that papa?"

"Both you, Sarah and you, Ruth, look just like your mama. You are so pretty just like your mama."

"Oh, papa, we must look like you too?"

"Oh, yes, but you get most of your looks from your mama. Let us get dressed so I can fix you your favorite pancakes. Sarah, go ahead and help Ruth get dressed. I think she needs a little of your help."

"Ruth, you have your dress on backwards! Here, let me help you!" exclaims Sarah.

"Don't forget your bonnets, girls," says Paul.

THE GIRLS MISS MAMMA

"Mama, we missed you this morning. Papa did pretty well in getting us up and making our favorite pancakes, but nothing like you do, mama," says Sarah.

"Papa can be extremely helpful to you. I would like papa to get involved with some of the things I do with you," says Delilah.

"Why, mama, where are you going?" asks Ruth.

"I am not going anywhere. Papa would like to be more involved with you girls, and me, well, as you can see with my big belly, I am unable to do everything with you."

"Mama, how did you get the baby in your belly? Papa says we were there in your belly before we were born," says Ruth.

"Ruth, you shouldn't ask mama that. It is not to be spoken of!" exclaims Sarah.

"That is O.K. Sarah. Ruth, in time when you grow up to be a big girl, I will explain all you need to know. Now, these chickens are hungry," says Delilah.

"Mama, Ruth gives the chickens way too much food," says Sarah.

"Let me show you Ruth. Take about this much of the chicken feed in the palm of your hand. Yes, that is it. Now, just spread it among the chickens. The chickens will take as much as you feed them. That one handful is enough for them right now," says Delilah as a tear rolls down one of her cheeks.

"Mama, the Community children say that your belly has a baby boy in there," says Sarah inquisitively.

"I believe the Community children are correct, Sarah. I truly feel you two girls will have a brother soon."

MAMA YODER QUESTIONS DELILAH

"Mama, I brought Sarah and Ruth, here, to spend the day with you. I have to see the doctor," says Delilah.

"Oh, gladly. I love the time I get to spend with your two little darlings. Has your husband Paul met with the elders?"

"Yes, mama, he has. He tells me he will be accepted into the church very soon. Paul will become one of us, in belief, rather soon. Mama, do you like Paul?"

"Delilah, dear, I do like your husband. He reassured me that he loves you dearly and he is taking care of you."

"Yes, mama, Paul and I love each other very much and I couldn't ask for a better man to be my husband."

"Are you able to cleave as much as you need, Delilah?"

"Yes, mama, we cleave regularly, and I am birthing children because of it."

"You know, Delilah, how important it is to cleave to your husband. It is in the Good Book."

"Yes, mama, we cleave every day. Paul is very agreeable, and he satisfies me completely!"

"Mama, I want you to feel comfortable around Paul."

"Dear, I like Paul. Why are you telling me this?"

"Oh, nothing, mama, I just want to be sure you like my husband and feel comfortable that he and I are doing our best for our girls."

"Delilah, you are starting to scare me. You sound as if you are pushing your motherly responsibilities off on Paul. Is everything O.K., Delilah?"

"Mama don't worry. There is nothing wrong."

UPSETTING NEWS FROM THE DOCTOR

"*H*ello doctor."

"Hello Delilah. How are you? Are you getting your rest?"

"Yes, doctor, whether I want to or not. I do get tired more often. It seems like I am more tired today than I was yesterday. My midwife, Rebecca, listened to my belly and says I have two boys in there."

"Lie down here, Delilah. Let me look at you."

"Doctor don't be surprised. My belly is quite big."

"Relax Delilah while I look. Yes, everything down there looks as it should. I am guessing you will be ready to birth in a couple of months."

"How do you know that doctor?"

"Your birth canal is starting to dilate."

"Is it too soon for that?"

"No, not really. I am assuming that you, being with child, is not stopping you and your husband from cleaving?"

"No doctor, it has not."

"Cleaving will start the process of dilating the birthing canal."

"Am I in danger doctor?"

"Under the circumstances, I would hope you two cleave as much as possible. Now let me look at your belly. I agree, your belly is quite large, and it looks as if you are carrying quite low."

"Yes, doctor, when I stand up and walking, I feel like I have this big ball weighing down on my hips. I sometimes will place my hands under my belly to keep it from falling to my knees, even though that will not happen, but it sure feels like it at times."

"Hmm."

"What doctor?"

"Just as I suspected."

"Suspected what?"

"Carrying your baby low in your belly sometimes means there is a full house in there."

"Full house, doctor?"

"Yes, I am guessing you have more than one child in there. Let me check the heartbeat. Relax, this is a little cold on your belly."

"Two baby boys! That is what Rebecca told me."

"Yes, I hear two separate heartbeats. It appears you will birth twins."

"Doctor, so far we have been talking as if I will…"

"I know Delilah. I was getting to that. I need to draw some blood. I must remind you that you are in grave danger birthing a child, or children as it be. You should not be in this condition with what your body is fighting. It is why I stressed you and Paul should not try for children at this time."

"I know doctor, but we are Amish. We are to build large families and I have an addiction to cleaving."

"Yes Delilah, I realize that, but under the circumstances it could be your life or even the lives of your babies."

"What happens next, doctor?"

"I get the blood work back from the lab and examine what has progressed. Besides your tiredness, do you feel any bone aches?"

"My legs seem to ache, but I attribute it to the extra weight I am carrying."

"Possibly, but more so that your bones are starting to swell due to the over production of the white blood cells."

"Will the pain get worse?"

"I am afraid so and more widespread to more of your bones. There will be a time when you will have a hard time bearing the pain. We can only hope you can make it to your birthing and survive that and only then can I try some treatment. I do not want to tax you or subject danger to your babies with treatments at this time."

"Can you cure me with the treatments, doctor?"

"I am afraid not, Delilah. All the treatments will do is slow the process and lighten the pain."

"I haven't told Paul."

"Delilah, here, take this handkerchief for your tears. You must tell Paul."

"I can't. I just cannot. It will tear him apart."

"Think how he will be torn apart when the time comes, and he isn't prepared for it."

TWINS

"Papa, where is mama this morning?" asks Sarah.

"Honey, she is resting," says Paul.

"But she is resting just about every morning and she doesn't do many things with us. She mostly sits in her rocking chair on the porch and looks at the sky. Sometimes she sleeps in the rocking chair and occasionally she will moan."

"Sarah, mama is ready for your brothers to come soon. She is very tired."

"Papa, you said brothers?" asks Ruth.

"Yes, girls, mama is having twin boys; they will be your new brothers."

DELILAH TALKS TO THE GIRLS AND GOD

"*P*aul?"

"Yes, sweetheart."

"Let me tuck the girls in bed tonight."

"Delilah dear, are you sure you feel up to it?"

"Yes Paul, I am well rested."

"Sarah, Ruth?"

"Yes mama."

"I am going to tuck you in bed tonight. Settle, now, under the covers and let me talk to you, O.K.?"

"Yes, mama, we love having you put us to bed. We love papa, but we have missed you," says Sarah.

"I know, you two. I have been very tired with these boys in this big belly, here."

"Mama, can we feel your tummy? Can we feel the babies?" asks Ruth.

"Yes, my little darlings. Here, place your hands right here and keep them there."

"Oh!" exclaims Sarah.

"Heh…heh," laughs Ruth.

"What girls?"

"We feel them moving, like they are kicking," says Sarah.

"That is correct, they kick a lot."

"Mama. This is fun," says Ruth.

"O.K., now girls, I want you to know how much your mama loves you. I want you to know how precious you are to me and papa. I am so happy you are my daughters. I want you to love your papa as much as you love me. When I cannot be around you, I want you to help papa like you help me."

"Mama, where are you going?" asks Sarah.

"I am not going anywhere. You will always have me near you, and we can always talk. Tomorrow, papa and I will take you to your grand-mamas for a couple of days."

"Why mama," says the girls in unison.

"Your brothers are about to be birthed and I will need you to be surprised when you see them for the first time."

"That is exciting, mama," says Ruth.

"O.K., now girls, always remember that I love you so much! Each of you give me a hug and a kiss before you settle under the covers."

"Mama, I love you and I want to be with you always," says Sarah.

"Me too, mama, I love you more than Sarah does," says Ruth.

"Ruth, you do not!" exclaims Sarah.

"Girls, I know you both love me very much and I want you to love each other and always remember that you are sisters; always help each other and remember you are family along with your brothers and papa. Here, each of you give me another big hug and a big kiss. Let us say our prayers, shall we?"

"Heavenly Father above. You are the vastness we desire, and You are our true giver, and we depend upon You for our strength. We thank You for the abundance of blessings You have showered over our family. My Father God. Please watch over these two little girls and the father who brought them into our family. Give them the strength to carry on in darkness; give them the light so that they may see. Give them the ability to understand that You are the supreme one who showers what is best for us. Lastly, Heavenly Father give my family

the strength to understand what cometh. I ask all of this in Jesus'
name Amen."

"Amen," says Sarah.

"Amen," says Ruth.

"Goodnight girls. I love you both so much," says Delilah as the
tears flow from her eyes while closing the door to the bedroom.

THE BIRTHING OF TWINS

"*P*aul, my dearest husband, please come to bed with me. Let us cleave and give thanks to each other, for we have each other forever."

"My sweetheart Delilah, I love you so much and I am looking froward to you birthing our sons. You are the mother of my children and to this I am so thankful."

"Paul, hold me, hug me tight and don't release me. Let us kiss so passionately."

"Honey, open up and let me enter…"

"Yes, my darling, do what you want with me. Enjoy my body as I will yours. I am so thankful for you, my dear husband."

"Mama, here are your lovely granddaughters. They are ready and willing to be of help to you for whatever you need. Paul and I will be at Rebecca's until the birthing is over. We will bring you over to see your new grand-babies when possible. Girls, give momma a big hug and a kiss. Always remember, mama loves you both and will always be at your side…always."

~

"Hello, Rebecca," says Paul.

"Hello, you two, I have everything ready. Mr. Yoder, you will have this room for the night and Delilah, you will be in this room with me for the night. The doctor is right around the corner if we need him. I am sorry, but the two of you cannot cleave tonight and must wait until your wife heals."

"Rebecca, I feel very tired, and I am a bit achy. The doctor said I was quite dilated and expects me to birth within the next twenty-four hours. I have been feeling pains down there and it feels like one of them is already poking its head out."

"Here, Delilah, lay down here. Mr. Yoder, we do not need you here. Please go to the bedroom. I will call for you when needed. OK, honey let me look. Oh, you are correct, you are dilated quite nicely."

"Rebecca, I don't know if I can do this. I am so tired. I am afraid I cannot push. Oh…oh…here they come…oh…oh…"

"Welcome to labor, honey. You have been there before. You know what to do. Your body knows what to do."

"Ahh…the pain…I feel, I feel like I have a….oh, my water just broke…"

Stay with me Delilah! Let me look and see how you are doing. Yeah, that is right, push those thighs open."

"Re…be…ca…I don't think I can do this…"

"You better do this honey! You have no choice!"

"Oh…oooohhh…ahhh…. oh…"

"That is right honey. If you feel like pushing, push!"

"I can't, I have no strength. It hurts to push, my…my…bones feel like they are going to explode. They aren't supposed to feel like that…"

"Spread them a little more honey. There, I see the top of the head, now push!"

"I can't, I am worn out. I am tired. I have no energy…"

"Yoder! Go get the doctor and hurry!" exclaims Rebecca.

"Father in heaven, I ask of you to take me before I lose the strength to live. Thank You Heavenly Father for all you have given to me…I release myself to You…," Delilah prays.

"Rebecca…I…can't…I have no strength to push…I am going to die….Paul……please, Paul, where are you?…."

"Honey, you better get pushing. Stay with me. You are not going to die! Now push…push…"

"I can't…I can't…"

"Doctor, she isn't pushing! She needs to push!" exclaims Rebecca.

"Delilah, listen to me. You must push in order to save the babies. Push and once I can grasp the head I will help, but you need to push to get the head out…PUSH!!" exclaims the doctor.

"Yoder get out of here!" exclaims Rebecca.

"No, let him stay! Paul hold her hand; comfort her; talk to her; let her know you are here with her," says the doctor.

DELILAH TIRES

"*D*elilah dear, I am here, go ahead and push; you can do it!"
"Paul...honey...I love you so much...tell them...the girls...I am so sorry, Paul my beloved...please don't leave me...no, Paul, please don't leave me...."

"Doctor here comes the head!" exclaims Rebecca.

"Delilah, this is the doctor...push...push!"

"I can't, I just can't...I hurt...I hurt..."

"Delilah, I have the baby's head in my hands, now help me...push as I gently pull," says the doctor.

"Rebecca be ready. I am going to pull the baby out and I want you to take it so I can get the next one. I am concerned the next one may be still if she can't push," says the doctor.

"Doctor, I think my wife has passed out!" exclaims Paul.

"Delilah, push...push...push..."

"Doctor, it is no use. She has stopped pushing," says Rebecca.

"O.K., Rebecca, I need you to push her thighs apart as far as they will go. I will have to reach in and hopefully get the head to pull the baby out," states the doctor.

"Doctor, I cannot open them any further," states Rebecca.

"I can't get to the head!" exclaims the doctor.

"Doctor, Delilah is still unconscious. What do we do?" asks Paul.

"O.K. all, help lift her up enough, so she is standing and leaning on the edge of the table. Hold onto her so she does not fall. Now, Rebecca, spread her thighs as far as you can, but make room for me to get in there. Yes, that is it! Come on baby, slide out for me. O.K., I got the head out, now gravity do your thing…yes, that is it. Easy, easy, yes baby, just slide out. Good, now take him Rebecca. Paul, help me gently place Delilah back onto the table," says the doctor.

MY DELILAH

"Doctor, something is wrong. Delilah will not wake up. She… her…her lips are blue! Doctor, she…she…is not breathing! Doctor, please help me! Make her wake up! Delilah…Delilah… Delilah," Paul wails and then weeps with his face lying on Delilah's cheek as his tears run out of his eyes and down his cheek until they meet with her cheek and meet with tears coming from her eyes, and united, they run onto the table. Paul lifts his head and places his lips on hers and kisses them one last time.

"Paul, I am so sorry. Did you not know?" asks the doctor.

"Doctor, I don't understand. What happened?"

"I thought she had told you. Way before she was with child, do you remember I was concerned about a condition appearing in Delilah's blood?

"Yes, doctor."

"I was concerned that if she became with child, the stress on her body could possibly take her life. She came to me inquiring about her condition of being tired often. I had found that the blood disorder was an overabundance of white blood cells in her bone marrow. I told her that the condition was not curable and terminal in a matter of time. It was at that time she told me she was with child."

"Why didn't she tell me, doctor?"

"I don't know Paul. I encouraged her to tell you. Maybe she was trying to avoid long term grieving that you would have had. I don't know."

"Doctor, did you know she would die birthing our sons?"

"Paul, I was praying to our dear Lord that the birthing wouldn't take her. He knew she would have to endure much pain the longer she was with us. He always knows what is best for us."

"Mr. Yoder, would you like to hold your sons?" asks Rebecca.

"Even these two angels from heaven look like my beloved Delilah," says Paul.

PAUL'S LAST TIME WITH DELILAH

"Doctor, may I have a time alone with Delilah?"

"Certainly, Paul, certainly."

"Delilah, my sweet love. Why did you have to leave me? I know if it were your choice you would still be with us. I want you to know I will always love you and cherish the beautiful children you have given to me. They will eternally be a reminder to me of you and your love. I miss you Delilah. I will be strong for our children. I will be sure they are well cared for with the help of the Amish Community. Delilah, sweetheart, I will have to leave you now, but always know that I will always be by your side, holding your hand, kissing your lips and forever caressing your soul with utmost care. I will always remember the times we have had which solidified our commitment to each other and lastly, honey, I will forever remember and feel our cleaving which formulated and maintained the eternal and unending loving bond between the two of us. Delilah, as we part, I am saddened by the huge emptiness I now feel from the loss of you, but at the same time, overjoyed with being able to have known you; of loving you; and the sharing of our lives together. Sweetheart, I love you and will forever love you for the rest of my life. Goodbye, my love."

FIFTEEN YEARS HAS PASSED

"Sarah, Ruth, are you about ready for the church group?"

"Yes, papa, we are about ready and finally have Jeremiah and Gabriel looking proper. Why are brothers so difficult at times?"

"You two girls look so pretty today; just like your mama."

"Papa, we miss mama so much. I know she would be right by our side as we walk to church, constantly primping our dresses; adjusting our bonnets, if she were with us," states Sarah.

"Yes, girls, I miss your mother every day, too."

"Good morning Elder Timothy. How are you this morning?" asks Paul.

"It is a beautiful day, Paul. We can thank the Lord for such a glorious day!"

"Yes, Elder Timothy, it is a glorious day!" exclaims Paul.

"Look at you two ladies; they look so much like their mama, and you two boys, I hope you are learning how to run the household," says Elder Timothy with inquisitiveness.

"Yes, sir, we are," says Jeremiah and Gabriel in unison.

"Papa, may we travel to the Community Center after our lunch?" asks Sarah.

"Surely but be sure to finish your barn chores before you go and remember to be back home in time to be ready for tonight's service; it will be a continuation of the lesson we heard this morning," says Paul.

WHAT WAS OUR MAMMA LIKE?

"Sir, Jeremiah and I would like to talk to you; we have some questions," says Gabriel.

"Sure. Come out to the porch and join me," says Paul.

"Sir, we want to know about our mama. What was she like?"

"Boys, your mama was a very beautiful woman and loved all of you so much."

"What did she look like, sir?"

"Your sisters look very much like your mama. She was soft spoken; loved life and an extremely hard homemaker. She was not afraid of anything, but very understanding of many things."

"We know you have been welcomed in this Community. Was our mama of the Amish Community?"

"Yes, your mama was Amish when I met her and for some time, she was shunned in the Community because she had married someone, me, outside the Amish belief. As you can see, the Community has taken us in as one of them. Just look how the Community has advanced to our home and now surrounds us. We are part of the Community."

"Sir, why did mama die?"

"Your mama had a blood disorder that is incurable. While birthing you two boys, the stress on her body was just too much and she passed unto the Lord when you were birthed."

"Sir, do you miss mama?"

"Jeremiah and Gabriel, I miss your mama every day and wish she were her with me; wish she were here to see how you have grown and I know she would be proud of the young men you have grown into."

"We wish we had known her too," says the boys.

"She is here with us. I know of it. I feel her presence. Some time, you need to sit quietly and let the outdoor breeze flow across your faces and you, too, will feel her presence. Talk to her; she will listen to you; she will shower you with her love. Take that experience with you everywhere you go, and you will be content that she, too, is by your side in everything you do."

MISTER PAUL JAMES MATTHEWS YODER

"*M*uch time has passed and as I sit here in this rocking chair where she would sit, and on the porch of the house I built for her, I dream of Delilah and I have missed her for such a long time.

Sarah and Ruth have grown into exceptionally beautiful young women and each have taken a husband, both from this Community. They have given me several grandchildren. Oh, how I wish Delilah could be here with them. Jeremiah had taken a wife from outside the Community, but in time, the Community accepted her, and she became the church organist. Gabriel had married later in his life. His wife is the widow of one of the younger Elders. They share two children from her previous marriage and they now have an additional four children from their marriage.

Me, well no, I did not re-marry. There could not ever be a replacement for my Delilah. I am not lonely. My children visit with me weekly and the grandchildren drift in and out during the weeks. I sit in this old rocking chair much of the time on this old porch that has stood so proudly all these years. I have gotten old; my beard is quite long, and I do not get around much anymore. As I sit here, rocking at a slow pace with a slight breeze flowing across my face, I close my eyes and she drifts into my vision. She is so beautiful and the glow of her eyes and the smile on her lips all glisten in the sunlight. With outstretched arms she motions to me to come closer. I hesitate for a moment wondering if this is just a dream or whether I am part of the dream, I contemplate for a short while and then I move towards her with arms outstretched to embrace her. As I come closer to her, I feel her hands touch me to draw me in and I place my hands on her hips. We pull each other in with arms clasping tightly. Our eyes meet with anticipation, as her face meets mine. She parts her lips as I part mine, and as they meet, I then realize, I have become a part of her life now, and we are together once again!"

THE END

ABOUT THE AUTHOR

James Roberts is an emerging author who writes stories of crime, suspense, thrillers and romance. This book is a fictional romance short story.

www.ingramcontent.com/pod-product-compliance
Lightning Source LLC
Chambersburg PA
CBHW051825170626
46807CB00003B/1037